Books by Tony Gleeson
in the Linford Mystery Library:

NIGHT MUSIC
IT'S HER FAULT
A QUESTION OF GUILT
THE OTHER FRANK
JESSICA'S DEATH
SOMETIMES THEY DIE

THE PIEMAN'S LAST SONG

The Tennessee Pieman was a beloved celebrity until he disappeared into seclusion near a small town. Now he's turned up murdered, his body discovered inside a garage on his ranch, and local police chief Wilma Acosta has assembled a bizarre list of likely suspects: employees who all seem to be harboring their own mysterious secrets. Despite her doubts about whether she's up to the task, if anybody can find the hidden killer among the perplexing cast of characters on hand, it will have to be the intrepid Wilma.

TONY GLEESON

THE PIEMAN'S LAST SONG

Complete and Unabridged

LINFORD
Leicester

First published in Great Britain

First Linford Edition
published 2018

A catalogue record for this book is available
from the British Library.

ISBN 978–1–4448–3889–3

Published by
F. A. Thorpe (Publishing)
Anstey, Leicestershire

Set by Words & Graphics Ltd.
Anstey, Leicestershire
Printed and bound in Great Britain by
T. J. International Ltd., Padstow, Cornwall

This book is printed on acid-free paper

1

If only Clyde Claudebetter had the good sense to die sixty feet further to the north, Wilma Acosta would have dodged a bullet, in a somewhat literal sense.

Wilma would have ample time to ponder that later, but when the mess all began, she hadn't a clue of what was yet to come. Another day was underway at the Amberville police department, and she had just entered her office when her desk phone started buzzing.

'Chief Acosta here.'

'Morning, Wilma. It's Will Marshall from the county coroner's office.'

'Good morning, Will. How's the family?'

'Everybody's good, Wilma, and how's George?'

'A half hour ago when I left the house, he looked so happy I couldn't bear to wake him to say goodbye. So what's up?'

'Wilma, you need to get up here. I'm at

the Claudebetter Ranch, and there's a problem.'

'The Claudebetter Ranch? Will, whatever problem you've got, you know that's outside Amberville town limits. That's the county sheriff's territory.'

Marshall cleared his throat. 'Well, actually, Wilma, here's the thing. You know how Clyde Claudebetter bought a hunk of neighboring property for his ranch a few years back?'

'I did hear something about that. So?'

'If you look at a map, there's like a little tongue sticking down into Amberville.' Will did seem partial to anatomical comparisons, part of his curious sense of humor. 'A small part of his property actually is in your jurisdiction.'

'That's news to me.'

'It was news to me as well. The sheriff himself is actually here, and he's just let me know about it.'

'What you seem to be trying to tell me is, something's happened up there this morning.'

'Oh yeah. And the sheriff wants no part of it. Since it happened in what's technically Amberville, he wants you to come on up in person so he can hand this over to you. The county crime lab folks have just showed up as well.'

'Lord, this doesn't sound good, Will. Just what kind of trouble is it that he's trying to hand over to me, exactly?'

'It's Clyde Claudebetter himself. He's been killed. They found him this morning.'

'Killed?' Wilma sighed mightily. 'All right, I'm on my way. I'll have a couple of my officers meet me there.'

'You know where you're going, right? Straight up State Road 86. The entrance to the ranch will be on your left. One or two of the sheriff's guys will be there. They'll direct you.'

Nightingale County Sheriff Dal Nickerson had a force almost a dozen times the size of hers. Of course he'd have a few men to hang around and direct traffic. 'Don't let the sheriff leave before I get there. In fact, *nobody* goes anywhere until then.'

'Nobody's going anywhere, Wilma.' Will had a relaxed drawl that always seemed stoically amused at whatever was transpiring around him. 'We're waiting on you. You're the woman of the hour.'

'Lucky me,' muttered Wilma, hanging up. She looked at the duty board on her wall to see who of her ten-officer squad was currently available. Luckily two of her best officers, Jim Burton and Clarence White, were currently in the field. She hit the intercom on her desk and asked the dispatcher to buzz them to meet her at the Claudebetter Ranch. She grabbed her hat and her almost-full coffee mug and headed for the door.

★ ★ ★

En route to the crime scene, she considered how little she really knew about Clyde, who was the closest thing to a resident celebrity that the area had ever been able to claim. She hadn't heard anything about him in a while now. Some years back, she recalled, he was a constant presence; on national television, across country-wide billboards and in expensive print advertising: the

Tennessee Pieman. He had started as an entrepreneur in his native Nashville, selling pies out of a family store that quickly expanded into a regional chain and then a coast-to-coast franchise. The biggest public relations asset was Clyde himself, charming the country in folksy commercials with his charismatic personality, down-home drawl and self-deprecating humor. You never knew what Clyde would be doing in his next ad spot: introducing his dog or one of his horses, picking a banjo or mandolin, or raking leaves before stopping to extol the virtues of his apple, peach or cherry pies, or especially his crowd-pleasing pumpkin pies. He ended every commercial with a warm smile and his trademark line: 'Y'all try a piece and you'll be back, hear?' The ads drew millions to his nationwide outlets.

A large corporation had bought out Clyde's business and made him a very wealthy man, but at a cost. He had to agree to abandon his public persona and even his famed tag line, which he was contractually proscribed from ever uttering in public again. He was replaced in commercials, advertisements and even on product packaging by an animated version of his own self. He became a recluse and one day purchased a large tract of land here in Nightingale County, almost two thousand miles west of his lifetime hometown. Wilma couldn't remember exactly how long ago that had been, but it was while her husband George was still chief of police, so it was over a decade. Rumors of an unhappy personal life cropped up but soon public interest in the Tennessee Pieman began dissipating. Local stories quickly dried up once it was clear that the new celebrity was not going to be showing his face around the area or hobnobbing with the locals. All of his business was conducted by agents or aides. The final rumors to be told, before everybody grew bored of talking about Clyde Claudebetter, were that he had not baked in years and had become a virtual hermit, spending his days with the things he had loved and now could own in quantity: horses, cars, musical instruments.

She sipped her coffee, deep in thought, as she drove. A washed-up celebrity recluse. A *dead* washed-up celebrity recluse. Not the type of thing that dropped on her doorstep as a rule. To quote a line from one of her favorite movies, she had a bad feeling about this.

⋆　⋆　⋆

Wilma had no trouble finding the entrance to the ranch. There was a high chain-link fence topped with a helix of razor wire running along the property abutting Highway 86, presumably continuing around the perimeter of the entire ranch. As predicted, at the opened gate to the ranch, two county sheriff's deputies were leaning on their police cruiser, presenting some small semblance of a deterrent to anyone entering or leaving the premises. Her department SUV came to a stop on the gravel, and they nodded to her as she rolled down the window. One of them — they seemed to be pretty much interchangeable as far as she could tell — approached the car and pointed through the gate.

'Morning, Chief. Through the gate and up to your left. You can't miss it. Everybody's up there. It's a real mess.'

'So it sounded. Two of my deputies will be joining me shortly as well.'

'We'll make sure they find you.' The man smiled and tipped the bill of his hat. The dirt and gravel crunched loudly under her tires as she drove through the gate, past an off-kilter and weathered old sign reading CLYDE CLAUDEBETTER'S FAMOUS PUMPKIN RANCH. The main road, its pavement in need of repair, continued uphill to the right to the main part of the property, but a newer blacktop drive spurred off to the left and up a smaller rise shrouded in pine trees. She headed in that direction.

Topping the short rise, she was almost at a small two-story brick building connected to a one-story brick garage. A large circular driveway, currently occupied by several official vehicles, fronted the buildings. A small knot of people gathered between the drive and the garage. As Wilma's car neared, two of them took notice and broke out of the group to meet her. She recognized Dal Nickerson in uniform, and Will Marshall in a dark blue windbreaker and jeans. Nickerson motioned for her to park in a space between vans marked with the insignia of the coroner's office and the county crime lab, and they waited for her to leave the car and join them.

Nickerson was a lean, dour sort, not given to smiling or small talk. 'Thanks for coming out, Chief Acosta. The crime scene is in the garage there.' He jerked a thumb over his shoulder to the four-car garage, whose two long articulated doors were both raised. She scanned the area outside the building: two more uniformed deputies, two techs in windbreakers identical to Will's, and three other techs were all bunched near one of the cars.

'Am I to understand that's Clyde Claudebetter in there?' she replied. Nickerson nodded somberly.

'Yep. It would seem he was murdered last evening here in the garage.'

'And explain, please . . . I'm being called in on this why, exactly?'

Nickerson pointed to the ground with both hands and stabbed his index fingers downward for emphasis. 'This here where we're standing is Amberville, Wilma. Clyde expanded his ranch some years ago with the purchase of an adjoining piece of property.' He jerked a thumb back at the road leading toward the entrance of the ranch. 'You saw where the old blacktop road branched off onto this extension? That used to be the furthest southern end of his property, and it lies not far from the line between Amberville and unincorporated county. This road here *just* crosses the border. These buildings here? This's your town, Chief.'

Wilma raised her own hands briefly in confusion. 'All right, we'll figure this out. I might as well go have a look at this.' She felt a spark of relief to see two police cruisers approaching down the same road. 'Sheriff, would you be so good as to fill in my deputies and have them come join me when they've parked?'

10

'Certainly.'

'And Will, why don't you walk with me? I assume you've finished your examination of the body in there?'

'I have.' He fell into step alongside her, hustling to keep up with her. For a large woman, Wilma moved fast.

'What can you tell me about this?' she asked.

'I figure time of death at around eight or nine o'clock last night. He was hit across the side of the head with something blunt and heavy. It fractured his skull, and then he struck the other side of his head on the pavement in the garage. Between the two impacts, he was likely killed instantly.'

'Dal seems eager to pass this one to me.'

'Maybe you heard about the recent dust-up he had with the city of La Paloma. Big turf battle over jurisdiction. He got burned in that one, and pretty embarrassed. I think he's just trying to avoid any more of that kind of hassle. He's content to stay master of his own domain here. The unincorporated regions constitute a pretty big portion of Nightingale County, after all.'

'And the fact he's up for re-election next year of course has no bearing on this.'

Will simply smiled.

They stepped under a string of yellow police tape into the garage itself. It held a late model Lincoln SUV, a Lexus sedan, and two classic American cars: a Ford Mustang and a Chevy Camaro. All looked gleamingly spotless.

Two lab techs, in jumpsuits and gloves, leaned over the body on the ground. One of them stepped out of the way to allow her and Will to pass. The other, a woman with long black hair pulled back in a ponytail, stood up and nodded to her.

'You must be Chief Acosta. I'm the field supervisor for the crime lab, Rose Flores.'

'Sounds like everybody knew I was coming,' Wilma said with a wry glance at Will. He seemed to blush a bit. She directed her gaze down at the body lying supine on the cement floor of the garage. After numerous years, it was still the recognizable face from countless bill-boards and television ads, with a full head of snowy white hair and bushy mustache to match. He wore a red plaid flannel shirt and khaki pants. His head was turned sideways at a severe angle, and there was a mass of maroon dried blood caked over his temple. A darker blob of dried blood had pooled beneath his head and soaked into the concrete floor.

Wilma crouched down near the body, resting her arms on her knees, and slowly swept her eyes over everything, taking in things slowly and methodically. 'When was he found?' she finally asked.

'This morning, about seven. The chauffeur was opening up the garage and there he was, lying alongside the Shelby Mustang.'

She turned to Will. 'And you say he was likely killed between eight and nine last night?'

'That's about right. I'll be able to give you a better time frame when I've gotten him on the table.'

Still crouching, Wilma cast her eyes

slowly around the garage. It was uncluttered and immaculately kept. She had never seen a garage so empty of any kind of detritus: no boxes, no tools. She stopped to focus on an object in a far corner.

'Is that a laundry basket?'

Flores looked where Wilma was pointing. 'Looks like it, yeah.'

It was empty, made of beige plastic, and it sat on the cement next to a closed side door. 'What's a laundry basket doing in a garage?'

'Good question.'

'Any idea where that door leads?'

'Someone said it's a small storage room or a laundry room. It's locked.'

'Be sure to print that, will you?' She resumed sweeping her gaze around the space. 'And I assume you were going to print all the cars, the light switches, and the doors leading out of here.'

'Sure. All the garage doors had been opened before we got here, so there's a chance of contamination, but we'll do it.'

'Who opened all the doors?'

'Must've been the chauffeur.'

Wilma stood up. 'And where's the chauffeur right now?'

'I believe he's in the other building,' said Flores.

'Any other footprints, marks, anything?'

'The scene is pretty clean, Chief. The only blood residue is directly beneath him. Not even a good set of footprints. We'll make sure everything's photographed just where it is, but there's next to nothing.'

Burton and White were slipping under the yellow tape, looking carefully so as not to step in the wrong place. They joined Wilma and she briefly filled them in on what she knew so far. She told them to speak to sheriff Nickerson about taking over the securing of the crime scene. They simply nodded and headed back out again. Wilma silently gave thanks that she had two responsible veteran officers on the spot; Jim Burton was, in fact, the senior deputy and her command backup. They would know exactly what to do in this case to keep the property closed off. She briefly imagined what it would have been like had one of her nervous new recruits been here instead.

Will cleared his throat. 'Sounds to me like you're okay about stepping in on this one, then.'

'I don't see as I have much choice. Anything else you can tell me right now?'

'Nothing that I won't be able to tell you better after we bring Mr. Claudebetter in for examination. What you see is pretty much what you've got.'

'Thanks, Will. Please get me photos and your report as soon as you can.'

Wilma stepped carefully around the garage, avoiding any physical contact with the cars or any vertical surfaces. It was the most barren garage she had ever seen: totally bare plastered walls and an open-raftered roof with fluorescent light fixtures. Even the floors were spotlessly clean, without even a grease stain. Besides the two long vehicle entry doors and the locked door behind the laundry basket, there was only one other door, which apparently led to the adjoining building. It seemed to be unlocked and just the slightest bit ajar, as if it had not closed all the way.

She saw Dal Nickerson outside, walking toward the garage, and she went to join him on either side of the yellow tape.

'So fill me in on what you know here, Sheriff.'

He nodded gravely and gazed around as he answered. 'We got the 911 call this morning around 7:00 a.m. from the chauffeur, Mr. Bivins. He routinely opens up the garage in the morning and preps whatever cars will be needed on any given day. He'd rolled up the doors when he found Mr. Claudebetter there on the floor. He says he used his own cell phone to call it in, and then sat outside in his own car waiting for the authorities to arrive. First I showed up with my deputies, then Will, and then the crime lab folks.'

'So the garage was locked up when Bivins arrived, and Clyde was dead on the floor inside?'

'That's what he said.'

'And this Mr. Bivins is where now?'

Nickerson pointed to the two-story brick building adjoining the garage. 'We had him wait in there, along with the administrator who runs the whole operation. We haven't talked to either of them. I figured out pretty quickly that this wasn't our jurisdiction and I had Will call you. So you pretty much know everything I do at this point.'

'What's the administrator's name?'

'I believe he said it was Moon. Excitable little fellow. He was chattering a mile a minute, getting in everyone's way, so I asked him to go sit in there and calm down.'

'Any idea why there's a laundry basket on the floor in the garage? It's perfectly clean in there besides that.'

Nickerson lifted his hat and scratched his head. 'Didn't notice that. Can't say as I've got any idea.'

'And that door it's next to, that's been locked the whole morning, is that right?'

'It was when we got here.'

They talked briefly for another minute or so, but it was clear that Nickerson had nothing else to add and was itching to pull his men and get off the premises. She thanked him and let him go.

'Don't hesitate to let me know if my

office can be of any help,' he said as he motioned to his deputies and they all made a beeline to their vehicles.

Right, thought Wilma.

* * *

The adjoining building appeared to be a 'secondary suite,' or what was commonly becoming known as a 'granny flat' or 'mother-in-law apartment.' Wilma walked across the driveway to a front door that opened onto a vestibule. A door to her left presumably led to the garage next door, and next to that, a staircase led to the second floor, where she figured there was some kind of bedroom. To her right, an open door led to a comfortable den with chairs, sofas, a conspicuous wet bar, and a large television screen on the far wall. Two men sat across from one another and when Wilma entered, both shot to their feet nervously.

'Are you in charge?' demanded the smaller of the two, a neat little man with glasses and a navy blue blazer. His voice was high and insistent. He walked toward

Wilma with agitation. 'What's going on?'

Wilma raised her hands. 'Calm down, please. I'm Chief Acosta of the Amberville Police. And who might you be?'

'Amberville? What about the sheriff? Where's he?'

'Right now we are actually in the town limits of Amberville, so I'm in charge. Now who are you, sir?'

The little man stopped abruptly and made a show of brushing the front of his blazer. 'I'm Marlowe Moon, Mr. Claudebetter's chief of operations. What's happened? Nobody will tell me anything! Was Mr. Claudebetter really murdered?'

'It would appear so, sir. Suppose we all sit down here and you help me sort things out, all right?'

'Are you sure the sheriff shouldn't be included in on this?' Moon sniffed, looking Wilma up and down.

'Sheriff Nickerson has departed the premises, Mr. Moon. As I said, I'm now in charge. Now would you *please* have a seat?' She gestured to the chairs.

'I really don't understand how this could have happened,' Moon fussed as he returned to his chair. The other man said nothing but calmly sat down.

Wilma settled herself on the sofa and pulled a notebook and pen out of her shirt pocket. She turned to the quiet man. 'And you would be?'

'Roy Bivins,' he said in a low modulated voice. 'I'm Mr. Claudebetter's chauffeur.'

In his own way he was as fastidious as Moon, close-shaven except for a small perfectly trimmed mustache, dark hair combed tightly to his head. The coat of a dark pinstriped suit lay draped over the back of the sofa; he wore a crisp white shirt, dark tie, vest and sharply creased pants. Both men gave her a mild case of the creeps and seemed out of place at an old ranch owned by a man who had once been famous for his down-home persona. Wilma turned to Bivins first.

'Do I understand you're the one who found Mr. Claudebetter's body?'

'That's right. When I opened up the garage this morning.' He spoke so deeply and quietly that she had to strain to listen. It was like he was speaking directly from his gut. It made her think of a teacher from her school days who ran the school plays and had them try to project their voice from the stage out into the auditorium. 'Speak from the belly, dear!' She shook off the memory.

'Are you the one who opens the garage every day?'

'Every day that I'm here, yes. I work five or six days a week, starting at seven. It's my responsibility to unlock the garages in the morning, inspect the vehicles, and then according to my day's schedule, bring out one of the cars and drive it up to the main house.'

'What about the front gate?'

'It's always locked. I have the code to open it.'

'So everything, the gate and the garage, was locked up when you arrived this morning?'

Bivins nodded. 'As usual.'

'How did you get here this morning?'

'I drive my own car and park it around the back.'

'Nothing was out of your usual routine today?'

'Nothing. I parked in the back, walked around to the garages, unlocked and opened the doors, and started to do my regular morning inspection. That's when I saw Mr. Claudebetter . . . ' He stopped and shuddered, his voice dropping even lower. 'I'm sorry. It was such a shock . . . '

'I understand. How long did it take before you saw his body?'

'Oh, almost right away, once I entered the garage. Next to the Shelby. At first I wasn't sure what I was seeing. My first thought was that a vagrant had snuck into the garage to sleep, as weird as that sounds. Then I realized it was him. I thought perhaps he'd fallen, but from where? There was no ladder; the walls have no shelves. I wondered if he was unconscious or what . . . '

'Did you touch his body?'

'Yes. Yes, I did. I bent over him and tried to speak to him, to see if he was responsive. I might have lightly shaken him. I don't remember. Then I saw all the blood. His eyes were partly open and blank. That's when I realized he was . . . ' Bivins did not finish. He stared down at the ground, looking dazed.

'And what did you do then?'

'I don't know how long I knelt there by his body; then I got up and ran back to my car. I'd left my cell phone there. I called 911 and waited for the police to come.'

'Did you try to call anyone else, like Mr. Moon maybe?'

'I tried but got his voice mail. I figured he was on his way in and would arrive shortly, so I left him a message to come to the garage as soon as he could.'

'Which I did,' Moon interjected, 'immediately after the sheriff had arrived.'

Wilma ran the scene through her mind. 'Did you move any of the cars in or out of the garage this morning?'

'No, I didn't touch any of them.'

'So let me be sure I've got this straight: Mr. Bivins, you're generally the first one on the property in the morning?'

'As I said, I'm the first employee to arrive usually, yes. I drive directly to the garage. There's an overnight caretaker on the premises but no longer night staff, except perhaps Mr. Moon.'

'I often stay later, overnight occasion-ally,' Moon said, sniffing, 'when circumstances dictate. Last night I wasn't here.'

'What about this building?' Wilma asked. 'Do you open this up in the morning as well?'

'No,' said Bivins, 'I don't have a key. It's a private apartment that Mr. Claude-better built for special guests. Sometimes he'd use it himself just for a change of pace.'

'And it's also where he housed his keepsakes,' Moon added with another sniff.

'Sounds as if you're getting a cold there, sir. Keepsakes, you say?'

'Allergies,' Moon replied with a man-nered wave of a hand. 'Yes, Mr. Claudebetter's original purpose in con-structing this building was to store the various items he acquired and collected over his long and interesting career. Rare cooking and baking implements, beer steins, automotive items, musical instru-ments . . . up until then they had just been stored at the main house where they couldn't be seen very easily. He also wanted a living space for guests when he invited them to peruse his mementos. He thought they might partake of his full bar into the late hours, as he liked to do, and should have someplace they could stay the night. That didn't quite pan out as he expected. He was known to stroll down here evenings to have a bourbon or two and look through his collection himself, and he'd sometimes sleep here.'

'And was Mr. Claudebetter here last night?'

Moon shook his head. 'I don't know. When I left last evening he was up in the main house and looked to be settling in. In recent times he's been much less active.'

'And what time was that when you left?'

'Around five thirty. I had some personal appointments.'

'So — forgive me, sir — there's someone who can confirm that you were not here last night?'

Another sniff and a fleeting look of disdain. 'Of course.'

'We'll follow up on that later.' Wilma

turned back to Bivins. 'And were you the last one to lock up the garage and leave last night?'

'I can't be sure of that. I wasn't here last night. I leave by one o'clock in the afternoon almost every day.'

'You're only here in the mornings?'

Bivins shot a sideways glance at Moon. 'Since my hours were cut back some months ago, my services only seem to be required in the mornings.'

Moon interjected hastily, 'We required some adjustments of schedules last year. Mr. Claudebetter no longer found reason to leave the property in the afternoons. He only wanted the services of a driver in the mornings. There were also some necessary budgetary cutbacks to shorten staff hours.'

'I lock up the garage when I leave,' Bivins said, 'but I'm hardly the last one off the property and I'm not the only one with keys to the cars or the building.'

'So yesterday, when you left, did you lock up the building?'

'Yes, around one.'

'Who else has keys to the garage, then?'

she asked Moon.

'Well, I do, of course. The caretaker. And of course Mr. Claudebetter has a complete set of keys. Generally there's no need for anybody else to have access to the vehicles.' He stopped to think for a moment. 'There's also a set of keys for this building in the main house, in case the housekeepers need to come down to change linens, vacuum and dust, or that sort of thing. There's also a laundry off the garage. They couldn't get keys to the garage doors, but they would have access to the garage from the apartment.'

Wilma thought about the empty laundry basket in the garage. 'Were any of the housekeepers here yesterday?'

'During the day, no, not to my knowledge. Possibly the evening house-keeper. She comes in around three and leaves around seven.'

'Only one evening housekeeper?'

'Budgetary concerns,' Moon sniffed. Between Moon's sniffs and Bivins' low mutterings, this fussy duo was getting on Wilma's nerves.

'Who else might have been in here last night?'

'The landscapers and the stableman left before me, but they would have no reason to be up here to begin with. The morning housekeepers were also gone. I saw they had all signed out. That's one of my duties before leaving is to check the roster sheets. There should have only been Mr. Claudebetter, the afternoon housekeeper and the caretaker.'

'That's all he had around here at night? A wealthy and famous man like Clyde Claudebetter?'

'For the past few years, Mr. Claudebetter has been rather a homebody, especially in the evenings. He didn't go out very much and almost never in the evening. Everything is locked at night. There are good fences and gates. We license a private security company to make regular checks.'

'I'll need to speak with the housekeeper and the caretaker.'

'As I said, the housekeeper doesn't come on until three. Purvis, the caretaker, is probably in his shack.' He punched the word 'shack' with disdain.

Wilma sighed. 'I'll need you to direct me to him, if you would. And I could use a list of all the staff here on the ranch with contact information.'

'Of course,' he said. Wilma braced herself for another sniff but it never came.

'And by the way, what's the name of the afternoon housekeeper? Is it possible she left the laundry basket?'

'I have no idea. It's certainly possible she brought some fresh linens or towels, but why she wouldn't take the basket back with her, I couldn't tell you. That strikes me as sloppy. Not good in a new girl. As for her name ... ' Moon snapped his thin fingers several times and stared at the rafters. 'Elaine? Eileen? Alena? Something like that. Alena Miller. No. Muller. I'm not sure. I'll look it up.'

'And ... how long has she been working for you now?'

'We hired her only a few weeks ago.'

'And you don't know her name yet?'

Moon waved his hand again. 'We have so much help here, and a fair turnover in housekeepers especially. Sometimes I lose track.'

No surprise, Wilma thought to herself, that there might be a turnover here.

She turned her attention back to the chauffeur. 'Mr. Bivins, you said you locked up the garage yesterday when you left around one. Did you also lock the door leading to this building?'

'It's usually not unlocked. As I said, the apartment isn't my responsibility. I tried it yesterday before leaving, and it was locked.'

'And I assume you didn't have occasion to unlock it this morning before you found Mr. Claudebetter?'

'No, absolutely not. I couldn't have if I had wanted to. I didn't have a key for it.'

'Excuse me a moment,' she said, getting up and walking to the door that apparently opened to the garage. Taking a handkerchief out of her pocket, she gingerly pushed it open. The lab tech was just on the other side, holding a fingerprinting brush. He looked up in surprise.

'Sorry,' said Wilma. 'Did one of you happen to open this door when you got here?'

'No,' said the tech. 'Nobody's touched it. This is how it was.'

'Not quite closed, you mean?'

'That's right, Chief.'

She nodded. 'Would you please make sure to print both sides of this door while you're at it? Thank you.'

'Yes ma'am.'

She returned to the nervous duo, both in clear anticipation of being dismissed and getting out of there. She sat down again without saying a word. They both sagged in disappointment.

'Just a few more questions. So neither of you would have any idea how that door between the garage and this building got unlocked?'

Bivins simply shook his head. Moon said, 'I can't imagine. I didn't come in here at all yesterday. There haven't been any guests lately. It may have been the housekeeper, or perhaps Mr. Claudebetter himself if he came down in the evening.'

'You mentioned the caretaker has a key.'

'Yes, I suppose that's also possible. But I can't imagine why he would have been here. Are you suggesting,' Moon said with another sniff, 'that the killer entered the garage through this house?'

Wilma rummaged in her pocket as she answered. 'That's certainly a possibility, yes, sir.' She offered the item she had found to Moon. He looked down his nose at it with surprise.

'You're offering me a packet of tissues?'

She smiled sweetly. 'Just thought it might be of help.'

'No thank you,' he replied coldly. But she did notice that the audible snuffling did not continue afterward. She returned the tissues to her pocket and her attention to her notebook and pen. 'Can either one of you venture any ideas as to who might have wanted to hurt Mr. Claudebetter? Were there any fights or disagreements, anybody who might have become an enemy of his in recent times?'

'*Enemy* sounds like a rather dramatic term,' Moon said. 'Nobody comes to mind. He could be difficult at times. He was a straightforward man who spoke his mind — set in his opinions and liked things a certain way. But he didn't tend to make enemies, as you put it. His very frankness and honesty precluded that. He didn't mistreat people or cheat them, which are usually the causes for enmity in my experience.'

'Mr. Bivins, would you agree with that assessment?'

Bivins considered that for a moment and said softly, 'Yes. I can't think of anyone who would have held a grudge for Mr Claudebetter. Certainly nobody working on this ranch. In fact he had very little day-to-day contact with most of the staff. Except of course, Mr. Moon.'

The glance that the two shot each other seemed rather nasty to Wilma. No love lost between those two. 'I'll need your contact information to follow up with you both. I'll also give you my business card so you can reach me if you think of anything else that might be of help.' She raised her eyebrows to Moon, who recited his office and mobile telephone numbers with an air of reluctance. She jotted them down.

'And may I assume you can be found here on the property during the day?'

'Almost always. I also have living quarters here for when it's necessary to stay overnight.'

'And where, sir, do you live when you're not here?'

'I have an apartment at the Hillman Inn, out on the interstate highway.'

Wilma knew the place. She nodded. 'And is that where you were last night around eight?'

'Are you suggesting I'm a suspect in Mr. Claudebetter's death?'

'Just trying to get a complete picture here, Mr. Moon.'

'As I said, I had some personal appointments last night. They were rather confidential in nature.'

'Should it be necessary, is there someone who can attest to your whereabouts, then?'

Moon's glare and tone of voice turned positively glacial. Someone seemed to have turned the thermostat down ten degrees. 'Should it come to that, yes.'

'Mr. Bivins?'

Bivins gave her his cell number. 'I live in a boarding house in Nightingale and there isn't a working land phone at the moment.'

'May I have your address in any case?'

His voice dropped even lower and he hesitantly replied, 'Fourteen-fourteen Skylark Road.'

'And I need to ask you the same question, your whereabouts around eight last night?'

Another hesitation. 'I was tired yesterday. I had an early dinner, went to my room and fell asleep.'

'So you were home all night then?'

'That's right.'

'And was there anybody who was with you last night?'

Bivins sighed deeply. 'No, I was alone all evening, until I woke up this morning.'

Wilma sat in thought for a long moment before continuing. 'Mr. Moon, I assume there were background checks run on everyone who works for Mr. Claudebetter?'

'Absolutely. We routinely did checks through a local agency.'

'And that would include fingerprint checks?'

'It would.'

'And you would have copies of these in your records I could see?'

'Yes.'

'Including your own prints and report, of course.'

'As a matter of fact, yes. But why . . . ?'

Wilma smiled and waved a hand in dismissal. 'Don't worry yourself. It's a simple matter of eliminating people who belong here. Maybe we'll get lucky and find a set of prints that don't belong.' She looked back and forth at them. 'Or you could come down to the station and get printed. It'd only take an hour or so.'

'I can supply you with the information,' Moon said frostily. 'And everyone's fingerprints, myself included, should be on your police database.'

'All right then. Mr. Bivins, I don't have any further questions for you at the moment, but I may need to contact you again soon.' She stood up and handed him a business card, noting that he took it with both hands and that they were shaking. She also noted the clean, careful, and somewhat odd manicure of his fingers — just what was it that struck her? — as he carefully inspected it and placed it in his breast pocket.

'Mr. Moon,' Bivins said, 'will you be needing me this morning or do you mind if I go home? This has been a trial.'

Moon actually turned human for a bare moment. 'No, of course I understand, Roy. You should go home today. Call me in the morning and we'll arrange for when you should return. I'll need your help for the preparations for the service and other things.'

'Thank you, sir.' Bivins rose, picked up his suit jacket from the sofa back, carefully folded it over his forearm, and nodded to them both, turning for the door.

'Mr. Bivins, one last question,' said Wilma. He stopped and looked at her. 'You're also Mr. Claudebetter's mechanic, correct? You work on all the cars here?'

'Yes, that's right.' Bivins looked confused by the question. Wilma just smiled.

'Thank you, I'll be talking with you.'

They waited in silence as Bivins departed; after a couple of beats Wilma turned back to the administrator. 'All right, then. Mr. Moon, I'll need you to get me what information you have on your staff and to direct me to the caretaker's cabin. You said his name was . . . ?'

'Chalmers. Purvis Chalmers. Go back to the main road and drive up about a quarter mile. It's a small wooden building with red shutters. You can't really miss it.'

'And then shall I meet you at your office?'

Moon sighed. 'Yes, just continue on the road to the main building.'

He stood, looking happy to be done.

'I suppose I shouldn't lock up this building until they're done out there?' Moon asked.

'No sir,' Wilma replied, 'you shouldn't.' She looked around the parlor. 'You said there's a memento room in this building, is that right?'

'Yes. It's upstairs. Why?'

'I assume you haven't been up there today. Would it be locked as a rule?'

'No, I haven't been upstairs and yes, everything up there should be locked.'

She reached back into her pocket and again pulled out the tissues, handing them to him. 'Could you just check upstairs real quick and see if any doors have been opened? Please try not to touch any surfaces like the bannister or the doors, and just try the doorknobs really gingerly, like, with one of these, okay?'

Moon shrugged, took the tissues, and walked in short, brisk steps out to the staircase. She heard his shoes ascending the hardwood steps and crossing the landing. A few moments later she heard him descending.

'As a matter of fact, both the bedroom and the souvenir room are unlocked,' he said from the doorway. He seemed to be hesitant to return to the parlor, as if he feared being hijacked by Wilma again.

'Don't do anything else right now, sir. I'm going to ask the lab techs to give it a once-over up there. I'll meet you up at the main building shortly. But I'd like you to come back here in an hour or two after they've left and see if you can determine if anything's out of the ordinary up there, anything missing or that's been moved.'

Another deep sigh, more sniffing, an irritated expression. But all he said was, 'Certainly. Shall I go get you that information, then?'

'Please. Oh . . . and you can keep the tissues.'

2

Wilma drove slowly back up the blacktop road to where it met the older paved thoroughfare. She saw Jim Burton standing at the entrance gate and they waved to one another as she turned onto the main road. There was already no evidence that the sheriff and his deputies had even been there. She stopped to consider that the entrance was back in Nickerson's territory and she could have argued that it was his job to cover the gate, but reflected that it wasn't worth arguing the point now. This way it was actually less complicated to run her investigation, and the sheriff clearly didn't care. Anything that made this mess easier was fine with her.

As directed, she found a short turnout ending at a rustic wooden structure with a shingle roof and fading red shutters. A tall red-haired man in a dark blue Pendleton shirt was stacking firewood against the side of the house and looked up as her vehicle slowed to a halt in front of the house. He finished carefully placing the cut logs and stood, hands on hips, as she stepped out of her car and approached.

'I'm Chief Wilma Acosta, Amberville Police department. Would you be Purvis Chalmers, sir?'

He nodded. He looked to be in his late sixties but quite fit, still possessed of a good head of hair, matching trimmed beard, and heavy eyebrows over piercing blue eyes that watched her intently.

'I need a word with you if I might.'

'I figured you would. Hell of a thing, whatever happened to Clyde. Come on in.'

The cabin was small and tidily kept. The front room was wood-paneled with a large stone fireplace and smelled of pine and cedar. Open doors seemed to lead to a back bedroom, kitchen, and bath. Chalmers motioned her to a chair. They sat across from one another and he stared expectantly, forearms resting on his knees.

'When did you find out about Mr. Claudebetter's death?' she asked.

'Marlowe called this morning, saying there were cops at the garage and Clyde was dead, and I should stand by for further word. Any idea what happened?'

'I was hoping you might help me with that, sir. It seems he was killed last night around eight or so. You were here on the property last night, were you not?'

Chalmers nodded. 'Yep.'

'Did you see Mr Claudebetter last evening at any time?'

'As a matter of fact, I did. We had dinner together up in his house around six.'

'You had dinner with your employer? Is that a common thing?'

Chalmers smiled. 'Sure. Clyde and I are old friends . . . the oldest. We go way back. I guess now I should say we *went* way back.'

'You knew him for a long time, did you?'

He had a deep, lazy drawl that Wilma found quite friendly. 'We grew up together back in Tennessee. Knew each

44

other since like, fourth grade. Always looked out for one another. In recent years, it was more Clyde looking out for me, I guess. I was kind of adrift. When he moved here to the ranch, he brought me along to set up and run his stables and to take care of various and sundry matters. Been here ever since.'

'So you were with him around six last night? Until when?'

'Maybe seven. We had a couple of shots of bourbon after dinner, talked about cars, and he said he might just turn in early. Then I walked back to the cabin here. That was the last I saw of him.'

'And that was up at his house?'

'Yep. Pretty common. Some nights I'd go up and have dinner and we'd play checkers or poker. Other nights he'd want to be alone and read or listen to music and I'd say good night and leave right away.'

'Was anybody else around, maybe the evening housekeeper?'

'Nope, can't say as I saw her. Just him and me. Clyde did the cookin'.'

'Did he usually stay at the house in the evenings, or did he walk around the property? Would he ever walk over to the garage or the apartment at night?'

'Now and then. He kept his collections down there, his souvenirs, and he'd get an urge to wander down to look stuff over, to head down memory lane. He has a good bar down there and he surely did love his bourbon whiskey, so times were he'd have a few, curl up on the couch and sleep there.'

'Were you ever with him when he did that?'

'Not too often. Clyde would get in a kind of mood where he'd want to reminisce, and once or twice he invited me down to join him drinkin' and rememberin', but you have to understand, he was a solitary sort for the most part. When he got in that kind of mood he was usually on a solo journey, if you catch my drift.'

'Sounds kind of sad.'

'In recent years, I think Clyde's memories were the happiest part of his life. He wouldn't get morose when he was like that. He'd actually smile and be happy.'

'Why do you think he went down to the garage last night? Was it to look through his memories, do you think?'

Chalmers shrugged. 'No idea. Seemed to me he was settlin' in for the night when I left him.'

'Was there anybody at the house who would have been with him?'

'Nope. The house was empty last night. There was just Clyde.'

'Was that unusual, for nobody to be there? Mr. Claudebetter was getting up in years, after all.'

'Damn, Clyde was healthy as a horse. He didn't really want a lot of people around. He was never comfortable with the whole idea of havin' people do things for him. Used to be, one or two of the housekeepers would hang around until late to make sure he had everything he needed before they left for the night. In recent years Marlowe cut back their hours and now only one is ever here late in the day.'

'Would that be Ms. Muller, I believe?'

'I think that's her name. Don't really know her, just said 'hi' a few times. She's only been here a few weeks now.'

'But she wasn't at the house last night when you left?'

'No, she had gone already. Like I said, the place was empty except for Clyde. He really didn't need her. I wouldn't be surprised if it turned out he didn't even know her name.'

'You're the caretaker here, is that right?'

'That seems to be my job description most recently. To be honest, Clyde's just kept me on out of loyalty in recent years. Not too much to be done.'

'So do you travel around the ranch to make sure everything's okay regularly, that kind of thing?'

'Yep. Check the gates, doors locks, alarms, all that. Not that it's necessary.'

'And you did that last night after you left Mr. Claudebetter?'

'Sure did.'

'Nothing out of the ordinary? The grounds were empty, everything as usual?'

'Yep. The gates were locked, the stables

were closed, lights were all workin' on the roads, alarms were workin'.'

'And the garage and apartment, they were locked up?'

'Uh-huh. It was all dark down there and the doors were locked.'

Wilma digested everything for a moment. 'So around seven or so, the garage was closed up, the adjoining building was closed and locked, and nobody seemed to be around?'

'Round about then, yep.'

'How long does it take to walk from the main house to the garage?'

'It's not that far. You could do it in ten or fifteen minutes easy.'

'And you've got keys to everything, right?'

'Sure.'

'Who else has keys to the garage and that apartment building?'

'Oh I don't know, let's see. Clyde did, of course. Marlowe. The chauffeur, Roy, has keys to the garage but maybe not the apartment. The housekeepers must be able to get hold of 'em to clean the building. Can't think of anyone else.'

'No other employees on the ranch who'd have them?'

'There are a few stablehands and landscapers who come and go. I don't think any of them would have any reason to have keys to the main buildings.'

'Any security guards who have access? Isn't there some outside agency that comes through?'

'Far as I know they only have the code to the front gate. They drive around and leave. To be honest, I don't think they do much good.'

'So why did Mr. Claudebetter hire them?'

'Oh hell, that was Marlowe. He does all the hirin' and firin'. He keeps tryin' to find ways to cut corners here and there. There used to be a few live-in regulars here on the property who would act as security among other things. He got rid of them one by one to save a buck. Tried to get rid of me a few times too, but Clyde wouldn't hear of it. To be honest, Clyde was not all that easy to get along with and he wasn't all that patient with the people who worked for him. He'd get annoyed easily and was only too happy to leave it to Marlowe to deal with them. But as I said, with me it was different. We went way back together. He may have been kind of a curmudgeon, but he was loyal.'

Wilma nodded. 'Sounds as if there's a big turnover of help here.'

'Well . . . Marlowe doesn't win any congeniality awards. And he's constantly cuttin' salaries and hours and generally makin' life hard for anyone who works here. Almost nobody's full time anymore; that way he doesn't have to pay benefits.'

'What about you?'

'My big perk is I get to live here. I get a little money but not all that much. When Marlowe couldn't boot me out he tried to cut even that back, but Clyde drew the line. So I think instead he cut Roy's hours substantially just to make a statement.'

'So I understand. The chauffeur only works from seven to one every day now.'

'Don't matter. Clyde hasn't had need of a driver all that much lately. Marlowe uses his services more these days, to go tend to business and save money on his own gas. Roy also details and maintains

Clyde's old cars and finds other things to try to stay useful. He even cleans the garage all the time. You see how clean it was down there? In any case, they didn't see any reason for him to be here in the afternoons anymore.' Chalmers rose from his chair. 'I've got a pot of coffee on. Can I offer you some?'

'That sounds good, Mr. Chalmers, thank you.' Wilma decided she liked this guy, and besides, he promised to be a more forthcoming source of general information about this place and these people than anyone else she had encountered. She might as well make the most of it.

However, she reminded herself, she couldn't eliminate him as an actual suspect just yet. Maybe he was a lot more charming than the other clowns in this circus, but she'd still need to keep that in mind.

'Afraid I'm out of milk right now,' he said from the kitchen, 'but I've got sugar if you'd like.'

'Just black is great, thanks.'

He returned with two dark ceramic

mugs and placed one on the table in front of Wilma. 'So you were askin'?'

'Frankly, not much of this is making sense just yet. Can you think of anyone who would have wanted to do harm to Mr Claudebetter?'

'Nobody. Clyde didn't exactly make bitter enemies like that. As I said, he could be abrupt and lose patience. He did not suffer fools, you might say. But as far as I could see, he had the respect of those who worked for him. What you saw was what you got with him.'

'But he could have been involved in an argument, maybe? It sounds as if he could be stubborn. Maybe an argument that got out of hand?'

Chalmers smiled and shook his head. 'Clyde could be stubborn, that's for sure. I haven't seen him come to blows over anything in many years though. When we were younger, sure. We both got in our share of fights back in Tennessee. But we both mellowed considerably.'

'Anybody else he was close with? Local friends? Family?'

'Clyde never made many friends

around here. When he first bought the ranch, he'd go into town to the supermarket or a store, now and then start up a conversation, but he was more comfortable keepin' his own counsel. He'd just send Roy or someone else on errands. I doubt there's any locals he kept in touch with. Family, well ... not anymore.'

'Not anymore? I don't follow.'

'There was his younger sister, Bonnie, but she passed away some years ago.'

'Wait a minute. His parents named them Bonnie and Clyde?'

'Pretty strange sense of humor, wouldn't you say? The Claudebetters were an odd clan. You'd have had to have known 'em. It gets even better: Bonnie's married name was Parker, like the famous gun moll herself! She married some third-rate musician who talked a better tune than he played. He was always on the road backin' up one headliner or another and one day he just stopped comin' home. So Bonnie moved in with Clyde and he took care of her and her kid, Stanley. He was like a father to that boy, especially after Bonnie got sick and died. He taught him to play guitar, ride horses, drive and fix his cars . . . even taught him how to bake pies. The kid had a lot of talent in all those areas too. He was smart and creative. Clyde taught him more important lessons, about being an adult and being true to yourself. They were inseparable for a time.'

'What happened to Stanley? Is he still around here?'

'Nope. They began to grow apart. He and Clyde came to some mighty disagreements. The kind of thing that happens as a kid starts to become an adult, think for themselves, find their own way?'

'Oh yeah, I know what you mean there, Mr. Chalmers. But that's usually just the normal bumps in the road of parenting.'

'Call me Purvis, please. It bothered Clyde a lot, that they were becoming less close. Anyway, there was something, I can't say for sure what, but it kept showing heavier and darker on him, and one day I came by and asked after Stan and Clyde said, 'He's gone and he ain't comin' back and that's the last we're gonna talk about that.' And that was the last we did.'

'And I take it Stan never did come back?'

'He surely didn't. He likely remained back in Tennessee, was what I figured.'

'How old was he when this happened?'

'Let's see, maybe nineteen or twenty by then? This was, oh my Lord, about fifteen or more years ago now.'

'And you've got no idea what that was all about?'

'Uh-uh.'

'And Stanley's never showed up here?'

'Nope, he hasn't.'

'And there are no other relatives, nobody else? Don't I understand he had guests at the ranch now and then, who would stay down at the apartments by the garage?'

'That was originally why he had 'em built, yes. I guess he thought it might be an opportunity to have some human contact now and then. There've always been business people comin' by to talk about buyin' or sellin' horses or a car.

Now and then someone would have a proposition to try to lure him back into a franchise. None of it seemed to interest him all that much, and over time he decided it hadn't been such a great idea.'

'He kept valuables down there, didn't he? Is there any chance that he might have showed one of those people something that they might have decided they wanted to come back for?'

Chalmers shrugged and raised his eyebrows. 'Seems a bit melodramatic to me. Thing is, nobody's been a guest down there for some time now. Mostly it's been Clyde spending time with his memories.'

'Melodramatic. Yeah, maybe I've been reading too many mysteries. My husband loves them. What kind of souvenirs are we talking about down there, exactly?'

'All kinds of stuff. Scrapbooks of clippings and photos of his early days with the pie stores, old ads that he appeared in. Some fancy cooking gadgets and classic pans and stuff. He hung around a lot with musicians back in the day, and he's got records and instruments. He was really into cars too, so there's all kinds of automotive memorabilia. And he's always been a bit of a connoisseur of good whiskeys. He's got a nice bar down there, with some rare old bourbons. Did I mention he drank a bit?'

'Yes, in fact you did.'

'So as I say, Clyde liked to have a few and take himself back to happier times. I don't think he was real happy of late.'

'Why do you think that?'

'Honestly, I think he was bored. Nothing presented much of an interest or a challenge to him. He'd tell me he'd allowed himself to get too comfortable. He talked a lot about old times, when he struggled to set up his bake shops and run his business. Wasn't easy. He was a good old boy and sometimes he was up against college-educated corporate types. But he beat 'em all.'

'I remember his ads on TV. He was quite a character.' She deepened her voice to imitate the way she remembered Clyde's commercial. 'Y'all try a piece and you'll be back, hear?'

Chalmers smiled. 'Now, that wasn't half bad, Chief. Yep, that was surely a big part of his appeal. He did figure out how to make some amazing pies, especially the pumpkin and the pecan. You took a bite of one o' those and you never forgot it. But what sold 'em across the country was Clyde himself in those ads.'

'How did the sale of his business come about?'

'It was unexpected. They came to him. You probably heard of Global Foods? They're actually a subsidiary of a much bigger international corporation. They were in the process of buyin' up a lot of smaller companies — diversifyin', as they called it. Clyde wasn't all that interested at first, but he sits himself down in a big conference room with a handful of these guys and his own lawyer and accountant, and one of these guys in a five-hundred-dollar suit scratches a figure down on a piece of paper and slides it across the table to them . . . '

'I never understood why they do that,' Wilma said. 'Why not just say the number? Guess that's why I'm a small-town policewoman and not a big-city CEO.'

'I never got that either,' said Chalmers with a smile. 'And neither did Clyde. But he took one look at what was written there and said, 'By chance did you put a couple too many zeroes down there?' and the guy shook his head and said, 'No, that's exactly what we have in mind,' and Clyde and his boys huddled and said yes.'

'He handed over his life's work, you're saying, for a bunch of money.'

'At the time he seemed pretty happy and downright relieved. He was never one for figures and reports and boardrooms. He liked playin' music, drivin' hot cars, raisin' horses, bakin' pies, drinkin' whiskey. He figured he could go do all that stuff without any distractions now. After all, he used to tell me, wasn't the whole point of goin' into business to earn yourself some money and some security? That was what he was bein' offered.'

'He seems to have had second thoughts after moving out here, if he built a guest house and thought about potential partners or starting up some new business.'

'I'm thinkin' Clyde was already gettin'

bored once he got here. And I reckon there are always people figurin' you're gonna catch lightning in a bottle one more time and they can hitch a ride with you, so there were plenty of people who searched him out with propositions. But he was always reminded how much he didn't like that kind of thing.'

'You said he used to do some competitive infighting, that sort of thing, when he ran his company. Any chance somebody like that might have come back looking for him, to settle some old grudge?'

'I can't see it. Clyde was a straight-up guy. He defended himself fearlessly but he never played fast or loose with anyone. He didn't cheat people. And he didn't really hold grudges himself either. It was live and let live with him.'

'Ironic choice of words, Mr. Chalmers. Somebody sure didn't subscribe to that as far as the victim was concerned.'

'Good point. But as to your question, I'd have to say there was nobody from his past who would've showed up and killed him, intentionally or accidentally.'

'How long has Marlowe Moon been running things here? Frankly, he and Clyde seem like an odd match.'

'He's a piece o' work, all right. When Clyde first moved out here he realized he needed someone with a different mindset to tend to the everyday nuts and bolts. I'm not sure how he found Moon, but there he was one day. The big thing he had going for him was that he was willing to take on all the things that Clyde found hateful and boring. In fact he kind of relished it.'

'What did Moon do before he was hired here?'

'I think he was in some kind of show business. Not that we've had any serious discussions about it, but I seem to recall he's mentioned livin' in New York, places like that.'

'Big-city guy. And he ends up running a ranch out here in the sticks. That's pretty curious.'

'I don't know that much about him, just that he's sometimes a pain in the neck and sometimes I have a much lower opinion, if you catch my meaning. You'd have to ask him about his background.'

'In your opinion is he trustworthy? Was he pulling anything behind the scenes on Mr. Claudebetter?'

'Nothing I could offer anything substantial on. Wouldn't necessarily rule it out. He's kind of a weasel, you may have noticed. Personally I suspect he's been trimmin' the operation around here to preserve the value. I think he's been figurin' it'd be his someday.'

'Was that Mr. Claudebetter's intention, to leave the ranch to Moon?'

'I got no idea. I'm sure he's got a will and all that spelled out. His lawyer's in Nightingale; you could ask him. Name's . . . let me think now . . . Stillman. Nate Stillman. He's been out here a few times.'

Wilma knew Nate Stillman; she made a note to look in on him. Her thoughts returned to Bivins, the driver and mechanic with the immaculate fingernails. 'What do you know about Roy, the chauffeur? Do you talk to him much?'

'Now and then. Mostly stuff like schedules and operations. He's not exactly an easy person to have a casual conversation with. He's been here about a year and a half maybe. Seems pretty competent. Good driver, good mechanic. Responsible guy, shows up for work and takes care of business.'

'You don't seem to have much involvement with the people working here, if you don't mind my saying so.'

Chalmers smiled. 'Nope. Like to mind my own business. Not too many people on this ranch I've ever really taken to, to be honest.'

'You don't seem to care much about how the ranch is run either.'

'No interest. My only concern was that Clyde was okay. Look, he basically brought me here to put me out to pasture, and I've always appreciated it. He didn't have to give me a job or a place to live, but he did. In return I take care of a few routine tasks around here, help out wherever I seem to be needed, and I guess I was the one person he felt he could talk to here, so I was sort of his sounding board and confidant.'

'Sounds like he didn't totally trust anybody else here.'

'Likely not. Paychecks don't guarantee loyalty and Clyde was no fool. He knew how far he could rely on someone and when to pull in the reins. I don't think he gave most of the people workin' here much mind, when you come down to it.'

'So as far as I can figure, the only people who could've gotten into that garage last night with Mr. Claudebetter were Moon, Bivins, and the evening housekeeper. Anybody you could add to that list?'

'Me, I suppose. And I got nobody to vouch for my whereabouts since I was here alone.' He held his smile and his gaze in the few seconds of silence that followed.

'In any case, we'll need a sample of your fingerprints. I'm sure you understand, so we can eliminate everyone who had reason to be there in case there are unidentified prints to be found.'

Chalmers continued to smile, and nodded lazily. 'My prints will be on record. Old Marlowe, I don't want to say he's a paranoid control freak or anything slanderous like that, but he insisted that everybody who worked for Clyde got thorough background checks including fingerprinting. That even included me.'

No love lost between those two, Wilma mused. She shifted gears. 'Any chance that somebody came onto the property that wasn't supposed to be here?'

'It's not impossible, but kinda improbable. You saw there are fences around the property and an electronic gate that's locked. That's the only way in, and you either have to have the code or get buzzed in by intercom from the main house or here. Did anyone say the gate was unlocked or looked tampered with?'

'No. Who has the code to the gate?'

'Roy and Moon both do, and so do I. Then there's the Mickey Mouse security patrol that comes through at night. Marlowe's not one to give it to too many, and he changes it regularly. The gardeners and the stable guys aren't supposed to have it; they have to be buzzed in. And the housekeepers — well, he wouldn't give them the time of day. They even had to scrupulously account for using the community keys to get into the other buildings. Anyway, if it was an outsider, they would've had to jump the fence or the gate and walk in. You might have noticed the razor wire along the tops of those eight-foot fences? They go all the way around the perimeter like that.'

'This place does kind of resemble a fortress, now that you mention it.'

'Yeah, well . . . when Clyde first moved out here, he was still high-profile. That's why he came out here, so far away, to get away from the notoriety and such. For the first few years he was awful sensitive about attention. I think that's another reason he hired Marlowe, to be a line of defense. Time passed and he became yesterday's news, but the fences remained.'

More than just physical fences, Wilma considered. 'I assume it's easier to get out than in.'

'Not all that much. If you don't have the code, you have to buzz the house to get someone to let you out. Or me.'

She closed her notebook. 'Anything else that might be of help here?'

'Not that I can think of offhand.'

She left another of her business cards on the table and stood up. 'If you come up with anything at all, don't hesitate to call, I'll be in touch. Thanks for the coffee and the help.'

'Wish I could be of more help. Can I ask you somethin'?'

'And what's that?'

'How long have you been police chief?'

'Going on ten years now. I took over from my husband, George. He was chief for seventeen years.'

'Keepin' it in the family.'

'Yeah, well, nobody else seems to want the job.'

'Policin' runs in your family, it would seem.'

'My father was a county sheriff. He thought I was crazy when I went into law enforcement. Generally it's a pretty good job.'

'I guess you don't get too many murders like this one.'

'No sir, and I hope that I don't get any more of them. My condolences on the loss of your friend.'

3

Back in her car, Wilma picked up her walkie-talkie and gave Jim Burton a buzz.

'Yes, Chief.'

'How's it going down there at the gate, Jim? All quiet?'

'The gardeners showed up for work. I checked them out and told them to stay away from the garage area. Nobody else has come or gone.'

'Do me a favor and give that gate and the nearby fence a good look, and tell me if it seems anybody might have messed with the lock or tried to go over the top.'

'Yes, ma'am. But I tell you, that's some pretty ugly concertina wire up top of that fence. You'd have to be some jackass to try to jump that.'

'Nevertheless, just give it a look, okay? And give the foliage along the perimeter a look-see as well, see if anything looks disturbed.'

'Will do. On first look up and down the

fence, there's plenty of bushes and nothing seems out of place. This would be one hell of a tough fence to get over. Excuse the profanity, Chief.'

'You're excused, Jim. I've heard the word before. Carry on.'

The drive to the main house was less than quarter mile further up the hill. Wilma was surprised to see that Claude-better's residence was fairly modest, a one-story Spanish-style home with red tile roofs and white stucco walls. As she drove up to the large circular driveway lined with low tiled walls, she saw Marlowe standing on the portico. He quickly stepped toward her car as she pulled up.

Hoping I won't get out and waste more of his time, Wilma thought.

'I thought you'd be here sooner,' Moon said.

'This is a murder investigation, sir. I'm trying to gather as many facts as I can.'

Moon lifted a large manila folder and offered it to her through her open window. 'Here are copies of all the applications and background checks of our employees. I took the liberty of including everybody who works here.'

Wilma took the envelope, unclasped it and briefly inspected the contents. 'Which is how many altogether?'

'Three housekeepers, two in the morning and one afternoon; two gardeners; two stablemen; Roy the chauffeur; Purvis the caretaker; and myself. That's ten altogether. I also assumed you'd want to talk to the security company that made the rounds here last night, so I included their contact information as well.'

'I appreciate that. And your own information's in here too?'

'Of course. I underwent the same process I expect of all my staff.'

'And everybody's been fingerprinted?'

'Yes. The service agency I use — you'll find their name and information on the reports — takes digital prints that are on national file. You should be able to access them through your official channels.'

Wilma leafed through the photocopied sheets and stopped at one. 'This would be the afternoon housekeeper, Alia Mulier?'

'Yes, that's her.'

'So this address and phone number should be current.'

'She's only been here a few weeks. I haven't had reason to try to contact her.'

Wilma nodded. 'Could I ask you to give her a call and ask her to come in, Mr. Moon? And in the meantime, are your morning housekeepers here now? Might I have a short chat with them?'

Moon seemed taken by surprise, and a little irritated, but he quickly recovered. 'Well . . . of course, Chief. Yes, they're both inside. You can park over there and come in.'

Wilma followed Moon through an open-air courtyard, past a tiled fountain, and into the house proper. He led her into a low-ceilinged parlor with sofas and extended a hand toward one of them.

'Have a seat, please. I'll send them in.'

She heard muffled voices from an adjoining room and two nervous-looking women entered, both in burnt-orange smocks and black pants. Except for their identical uniforms, they couldn't have been more different. One was perhaps in her forties, with braided blonde hair, while the other looked in her early twenties with deep black hair and dark skin. Moon followed them in, said, 'Chief, this is Birgitta and Elizabeth. I'll go make that call now,' and was gone again. Wilma smiled at the two and said, 'Please, sit down, ladies. I just have a few questions for you.'

Their discomfort was almost tangible. Wilma decided she needed to set them at ease. 'I'm Wilma Acosta, chief of police of Amberville Township. Could you tell me your names, please?'

The blonde spoke up first. 'I'm Birgitta Hansen. I've worked for Mr. Claudebetter for over a year now. This is terrible, what's happened.'

'Yes, ma'am. I'm here to try to figure out exactly what did happen. And you, ma'am?'

The younger lady said, 'My name is Elizabeth Soriano. I've worked here for about eight months.'

'It's my understanding that neither of you were here last night when Mr. Claudebetter died, is that correct?'

'Yes,' said Birgitta Hansen. 'We both

left at one o'clock yesterday afternoon.'

'You both only work in the mornings and there's an afternoon housekeeper?'

'That's correct. When I first came here, I worked all day, but the shifts were shortened. We now work from eight until one five days a week.'

'Have you gotten to know the afternoon housekeeper — her name is Alia, right?'

Birgitta shrugged. 'She hasn't been here very long. We're usually gone before she ever comes in. I haven't really had a conversation with her.'

Wilma turned to look at Elizabeth.

'We talked a couple of times when I happened to be here late, but it's like, what do you call it, ships passing? She'd be coming and I'd be going, and I'd be in a hurry because I was late. She didn't seem very talkative.'

'Do all of you have occasion to go down to the apartment by the garage?'

'Oh yes,' replied Birgitta. 'We regularly clean the apartment and change the linens and towels. Mr. Moon requires that they be changed every week.'

'I thought there weren't many visitors anymore. Are there regular occupants there that the linens and towels need to be changed?'

'Not of late, but Mr. Claudebetter often would spend the night there, so Mr. Moon wanted to be sure the place was maintained.'

Wilma nodded thoughtfully. 'How's that work? Where do you do the laundry and where do you keep the new linens and towels?'

'We keep the linen closets stocked at the apartment, upstairs. There's a washer and dryer off the garage, in a side room. Usually, anyway.'

Wilma thought about the locked door and the laundry basket. 'What do you mean by 'usually'?'

'Well, the washing machine hasn't been working for a few days now. They've been trying to get a repair man out here, but this week we'd have to bring the laundry up to the washers in the main house here, and bring back the clean linens and towels.'

Wilma smiled. 'I know how that works.

Washer breaks down just when you need it the most, huh? When did you discover it was broken?'

Birgitta and Elizabeth looked at each other and shook their heads. Elizabeth turned back to Wilma. 'It wasn't either one of us. We heard about it from Mr. Moon.'

'Maybe it was Alia?' Birgitta said.

'So . . . have any of you had to bring the apartment laundry up or back this week?'

Again they both shook their heads. 'Maybe Alia,' said Elizabeth.

'Let's suppose you did have to bring laundry up here or back right now. How would you do it? Would you drive a car down there?'

'Oh no,' said Birgitta. 'It's not very far to walk, and the weather's good. We'd have just carried a basket down. There's not a lot that would have to be brought back. The baskets are light too.'

'I know this is kind of a strange question, ladies, but . . . what kind of laundry baskets do you use?'

'They're about this big,' Birgitta said,

extending her hands apart. 'They're plastic. As I said, very light.' She looked at Wilma quizzically.

'And let me guess, they're kind of a tan or beige color?'

'Some of them, yes.'

'Okay, thank you. I appreciate your help.' Wilma rose from the seat and hesitated. 'Alia must have talked to *somebody* since she's been working here. Would there be anyone here who might have gotten to know her better, perhaps?'

Both women shook their heads. 'Working up here, we don't leave the house itself all that much and don't get to talk to a lot of people,' said Birgitta. 'Mr. Moon mostly, when he gives us our daily instructions. And of course Mr. Claudebetter . . . may he rest in peace.'

'Mr. Chalmers sometimes,' offered Elizabeth. 'He spends some time up here in the house with Mr. Claudebetter. He's a very nice man, always very polite to us.'

Wilma considered asking about their relationship with Marlowe Moon but at that moment he re-entered the room.

'I've been unable to get hold of Ms.

Mulier,' he said. 'I'm just getting her voice mail. I've left a message for her to return my call and to come in as soon as possible.'

'Thank you, sir. Please let me know as soon as you hear from her.' She turned to the women and said, 'And thank you for your time, ladies. I've got no further questions for you.' They both stood and nodded, still looking uneasy.

'If there's nothing else, then,' sniffed Moon, 'I'll see you to the door.'

When they reached the courtyard, Wilma said, 'They both look very upset by Mr. Claudebetter's death. You might want to give them the rest of the day off.'

Moon nodded. 'You're right. I see no reason to keep them around today.'

'I'll make sure you know when Ms. Flores says you can return to the garage and the apartment and check everything for me, okay?'

'That would be fine. You've got my cell phone number.'

'One final question for now, Mr Moon. To your knowledge, has anyone out of the ordinary tried to contact Mr. Claudebetter recently?'

Moon frowned. 'Out of the ordinary?'

'Maybe unusual phone calls or mail?'

'Postal mail? We almost never get any. We do get lots of telemarketers. Sales calls. Scams. Pranksters. Everybody does. The phone has turned into a nuisance appliance in recent years.'

'But nothing of a more personal nature, someone who clearly knew Mr. Claudebetter, let's say? Someone who would have asked for him by name or maybe even spoken to him?'

'It's probably not even worth mentioning, but there was that crazy woman who called, oh, it must be over a month ago now. She claimed to be a relative of his and insisted on being put through to him. She said it was a matter of the utmost urgency. It sounded like a scam. I refused to let her speak to him.'

'A relative, you say?'

'She said she was his niece or something like that, but that's nonsense. Claude has no close relatives except for a nephew, whom he hasn't seen in years, and this clearly was *not* him. There are no other close relatives whatsoever, and certainly no female relatives. It was a phone scam, as much as the fake IRS agents or the home repairmen who knew his name as well.'

'And she called the main landline, not Mr. Claudebetter's cell phone?'

'Mr. Claudebetter never had a cell phone. He didn't believe in them. He always said he came out here to get away from people, not to be easier to find.'

'Any record of those calls, where they came from?'

'No. Our land line stores the numbers of about fifty past callers but that one's been cycled through by now.'

'And there's nothing else you could recall about the caller, like her voice or anything specific she said?'

'She said her name was . . . Stacy or Stephanie or something like that; I don't remember. I don't even know why I mentioned it. It probably means nothing. Are we done here?'

'For now, yes sir. I'll talk to you later after you've had the chance to inspect the apartment and the garage.'

She couldn't hear what he muttered under his breath as she left, but she could swear he said, 'I can't wait.'

She gave Clarence White a quick buzz on the intercom as she got into her vehicle. 'How's it going down there?'

'All smooth, Chief. They've just bagged the body and are in the process of removing it to the morgue. The lab techs will likely be here for a while yet. They're being pretty thorough.'

'That's good. Do me a favor, if you will. I'm going to text you the cell number of the property administrator, Marlowe Moon. He's going to need to head down there to do an inspection of the premises when he won't be in the way, so would you call him when the lab folks are done?'

'You got it, Chief.'

'It looks as if Jim's deflecting any incoming traffic from there, so you shouldn't have any trouble maintaining the crime scene. It's okay to let Moon into the buildings but keep everybody else out for the moment. Let me know if anything comes up. I'm going to look around here a bit before I take off.'

'Yes, ma'am.'

Wilma closed her phone and gunned her engine. Good men, those two, and good cops. She just wished they'd loosen up just a little. She wasn't sure she liked being called 'ma'am.'

It bothered her that Alia Mulier couldn't be reached, but she decided it was still a little early for major concern. She worked afternoons; maybe she slept in and turned her phone off. On the other hand, she was the one person that had been in the building last evening that wasn't yet accounted for. Wilma decided to bide her time for a little while yet before sending someone out to search Ms. Mulier down.

Wilma drove a short distance and stopped. She got out of her vehicle and surveyed the landscape. The main house was on the highest vantage point of the ranch, and from here she could pretty much see the entire property. It looked to be perhaps a few thousand acres, not a huge property but decent. Oaks, pines and sycamores covered the area except for the horse paddocks near the stables, but she could see most of the surrounding high perimeter fence, topped with razor wire. Access to the ranch was not easy.

Her concentration was broken by a sound further down the road: the clopping of hooves. It was a sound that brought back memories; Wilma had always loved horses and had owned a couple in earlier years. She turned to see a figure in a cowboy hat and yellow shirt astride a lovely palomino stallion making a leisurely pace towards her. As he approached, she realized the rider looked familiar.

'Diego!' she called out. 'Diego Fuentes! Is that you?'

When he was about twenty feet away, the man smiled and tipped the brim of his hat. 'Wilma! Well, I'll be. What are you doing here?'

'Are you trying to tell me you didn't know there was a murder up here?'

He pulled up his horse, who gave a low snort. 'Oh sure. We all heard the news about Mr. Claudebetter this morning. Terrible thing. But I didn't know you'd be involved in it. You're still down in Amberville, aren't you?'

'Seems Mr. Claudebetter got himself killed within my jurisdiction.' She was getting tired of explaining that. 'So I could ask you the same question: what are you doing here? I haven't seen you in years. Last I recall, you had a nice setup with that big breeding stable up north.'

His saddle creaked as Fuentes leaned forward, took off his hat and wiped his forehead with the back of his hand. His curly hair was still full and dark, with some salt creeping into the pepper. His English was perfect but he still had the softest trace of his Michoacán accent. 'Yeah, the thing with the breeders didn't work out.'

'Sorry to hear about that.'

Fuentes shrugged. 'They made some bad decisions and filed for bankruptcy. They let a lot of us go. But the owner liked me. She'd heard the ranch here was hiring stablehands and gave me a good reference.'

'So how long have you been here?'

'Over five years now. It's a good job. I spend more time with the horses than with people. That's always appealed to me. And they're nice horses.' He shook his head. 'A real shock, that something like this could happen to the old man. He was a decent sort, I guess.'

Wilma remembered that Diego Fuentes had always been a plain-spoken man. His lack of sentimentality didn't surprise her. 'How well did you get to know Mr. Claudebetter?'

'Not well at all. He'd come down to ride one of his horses or just spend time with them, but he'd ignore the people. He and I would talk about his horses now and then, of course. We'd talk about their health, feeding, exercise, and so on. More often I'd just get instructions secondhand through his *pequeño ayudante*.'

His 'little helper.' Wilma caught the undertow in his use of the Spanish words. There didn't seem to be any love lost between Moon and anybody who worked here, she considered.

Fuentes sat thoughtfully for a moment,

leaning on the saddle horn, before continuing. 'I know it must sound kind of weird, but it's like I never felt any kind of connection to the guy. I don't really think they gave a thought to those of us who work here. Claudebetter was off in his own distracted world. His *helper* always talked to us like we weren't really there. I'd be willing to bet that neither one of them could have told you our names or what we looked like or anything. It's a strange place to work. We pretty much got left alone as long as we did our jobs and kept things running smoothly, which wasn't all that hard.' He gently patted the neck of the palomino. 'Now, it's a different story with Sugarcane, here. We're great friends, and that goes for all his brothers and sisters back at the corral. This is why I love my job.'

'So it sounds like there's not much you can tell me about Mr. Claudebetter or the other folks who work with him.'

'I'm afraid not. As I said, it's a strange place to work. I don't get the feeling anybody really knows anybody else here. There's Benny and me down at the paddock, and we spend all our time with the horses. The groundskeepers come and go like dust in the wind.'

'Do you ever talk to the chauffeur or any of the housekeepers?'

Fuentes shook his head. 'Nope. Now and then Purvis Chalmers comes down because he likes the horses. We exchange small talk. He doesn't seem to be much of a talker.'

'Really? That's a surprise. I couldn't get him to shut up just now.'

'Yeah, well ... he's always been friendly enough, just distant.' He stared out at the vista. 'I don't want to say it's got anything to do with Benny and me being Mexican, but maybe. More likely it seems to me more that everyone who works here is just plain loopy. There's a saying in Spanish: *cada mente, otro mundo*. That means 'Each mind, its own world.' They're all in their own worlds, you know what I mean?'

'I think I'm beginning to, yes.'

'This ranch is like a big poker game, and everybody's playing their cards close to their vests. And, well, maybe I'm talking out of school here, but . . . '

'Go ahead, Diego.'

'Well . . . that Moon character, there's something else about him. He strikes me as not all here, you know? He's always nervous and edgy, kinda fussy and paranoid. I don't want to make accusations I can't back up, but maybe he's on something. Anyway, it just seems he's not always paying attention to things. Anyhow, whatever might be going on, it's up here on the hill and doesn't reach us down there.'

Wilma nodded. 'I understand what you're saying. This conversation won't go any further than you and me. I appreciate your frankness.'

Fuentes sat up in the saddle and grasped the reins. 'I better be getting Sugarcane back to the stable. I have to give a couple of the mares their day's exercise as well. I doubt I can be of much more help to you on this one, but feel free to call on me if you think I can.'

'I'll keep that in mind. Good to see you, Diego.'

'Lots of luck, Wilma. I have a feeling

any answers you're seeking won't come easy, with this crew.'

Diego Fuentes rode his palomino back down the road and Wilma returned to her vehicle, shaking her head. She figured he had pegged this one just right.

★　★　★

Wilma decided to take the short drive to Nightingale and pay a visit to the lawyer, Nate Stillman. Exiting the front gate of the ranch, she saw that Jim Burton was having an intense discussion with someone in a television news van from local Channel 6. It hadn't taken very long for the word to get out. Nickerson, she thought, or someone in his office, had dropped a word. Or maybe someone from the station had simply been hanging out hoping to pick up something like this.

She stopped her vehicle, got out and walked over to the driver's side of the van. The male driver and female passenger were animatedly chattering at Jim, who was stoic behind his aviator sunglasses, his hands on his hips.

'Chief Acosta!' yelled the blonde woman in the passenger seat. Wilma recognized her as Holly Travers, the evening news reporter. 'What's going on in there? We need to get in and see!'

Wilma forced a smile, tipped back her hat, and leaned in to the window. 'Morning, Ms. Travers. Right now it's a crime scene and it's closed off to the public. We can't let you in just yet.'

'Is it true that Clyde Claudebetter was murdered?'

'Mr. Claudebetter is dead. For the moment that's all I can tell you. We're currently investigating. If you contact my office later this morning, I'll have more information for you.'

'Why is your department investigating this and not the sheriff?' Travers demanded, still shouting. She was holding a microphone of some sort across the driver toward the window.

'It's fallen under our jurisdiction, ma'am. I can't tell you anymore right now until I know more myself. I can't let you come into an active crime scene. If you could please come to the police department at, let's say, noon, I'll give you a full briefing.'

Travers considered that for a moment, not looking very happy, and then told the driver, 'Okay, we'll shoot me from out in front of the gate then.' As the van backed out onto the shoulder, Wilma and Jim exchanged glances.

'Anybody else try to come through?' she asked.

'The coroner's van just left. That was it.'

'Might be more news people. Better close the gate up,' she told him. 'Nobody in or out except the staff.' Jim nodded. She returned to her car and drove out, watching in her rear-view mirror as her deputy rolled the gate shut. Holly Travers and her driver, who was also her cameraman, were already getting out of the van to position themselves to record her in front of the closed gate.

Good lord, Wilma thought, *this is just what I need this morning.* She accelerated down the highway toward Nightingale.

She picked up her two-way and buzzed Natalie, the adjutant and communications officer at the department.

'How's it going up there, Chief?'

'It's surely going. Any news over there?'

'We got a call from Channel 6 with questions about the Claudebetter ranch. I told them you'd get back to them.'

'Heads up, Natalie. I'm trying to keep them happy for the moment so we'll have a free afternoon to deal with the evidence that should be coming in. I need you to prepare for a quick news conference at noon. Think you can do that?'

'A news conference! Wow! That's exciting!'

'Lord save us all from exciting. Can you make all the arrangements and just keep tight-lipped until I get there? Better call Channel 10 over in Staughton and inform them as well. Contact the Nightingale newspaper too. We don't want to look like we're favoring or excluding anyone. If anybody else calls from any media, just tell them to be there at noon. Be courteous and official but not very helpful.'

'Leave it to me. When will you be back?'

'One stop in Nightingale, then I'll be there.'

'I'll stonewall 'em until you get here, Chief. I always wanted to say that.'

Wilma signed off, shaking her head and smiling. Natalie was young, but she was focused and had always been good under pressure. She'd come through just fine. Whether Wilma herself would was another question; this was brand new territory for her. She silently cussed Dal Nickerson under her breath as she drove.

* * *

'Well, Chief,' Nate Stillman said, 'Come on in. It's been a long time.' He stepped back and waved her into his office.

Wilma knew Stillman from court cases. He had frequently defended locals for offenses such as driving under the influence, and occasionally showed up to plead for someone accused of something more serious such as a burglary or assault. Of late she hadn't had much

93

cause to appear personally in court, so they had not crossed paths in a year or two.

'Still taking on the DUI cases?' Wilma smiled as she sat down across the desk from Stillman.

'I'm not in court all that much anymore. More administrative law these days. My daughter's an attorney now and I send a lot of that kind of thing her way. She's doing a nice job too.'

'I tend to stay out of the courtrooms myself of late,' Wilma replied. 'This is a friendlier encounter than those old days.'

'So how can I help you?'

'You probably haven't yet heard the news, but Clyde Claudebetter was found dead this morning out at his ranch.'

'Oh no! I hadn't heard. What happened?'

'It's under investigation, but it looks like homicide.'

'The devil you say! I just spoke with Clyde about two or three months ago, out at the ranch.'

'Did you take care of much legal work for him?'

'Just occasional things. When he purchased the neighboring tract of land . . . preparation of official documents like that.'

'I understand you helped draw up his will.'

'Yes, I did.'

'Can I ask you some questions about it?'

Stillman hesitated. 'A murder case, you say? Someone killed Clyde?'

'It certainly seems so, yes.'

He expelled a long breath. 'What would you like to know?'

'For starters, who's mentioned in the will?'

'Well, there don't seem to be next of kin. No relatives he ever mentioned at all. The ranch itself, real estate and livestock, go to Purvis Chalmers. There's provision for payment of any outstanding debts. There's a piece, not gigantic but reasonable, left to his administrator, Marlowe Moon. He's also named as the executor. Chalmers gets a sizable part of the remainder, along with select charities.'

'What about his cars, the other items

he's collected? I understand they're of some value.'

'Yes, there's mention of other effects, as he lumped them together. They're all to be sold at auction and the proceeds added to the liquid assets for distribution.'

'And that's it?'

'It would seem there's not much more.'

'And nobody else is mentioned in his will but Chalmers and Moon?'

'There really is nobody else.' Stillman spread his hands. 'If you're asking about the rest of his staff, nobody else's name ever came up in our conversations.'

'Perhaps you'll view this as an intrusion on the attorney-client privilege, but I have to ask. Was there anything else he discussed with you that might have a bearing on this? Any animosities, disagreements, that sort of thing?'

'There's nothing I'd need to protect in any case. All the dealings I had with him were pretty routine. I helped him cross the T's and dot the I's and that was it. There were no lawsuits or legal confrontations. It would seem Clyde's major concern was to protect his privacy and lead his life.'

'And his privacy was never an issue? Nobody tried intruding upon it as far as you know?'

Stillman sat back and bridged his fingers. 'As in restraining orders, inter alia? No. Never.'

'Excuse me, sir, 'inter alia'?'

He smiled slightly. 'Forgive me, I'm lapsing into lawyer-speak there. 'Inter alia' means 'among other things.' It's that Jesuit education. I had four years of Latin and it's a shame to have it go to waste. I guess I can be a little pompous at times.'

Kind of the way she remembered him, Wilma reflected. But she simply smiled back. 'Is there any kind of list of his effects, as you call them, included in the will?'

Stillman shook his head thoughtfully. 'No. He didn't itemize anything. He simply said anything to be found that was not real estate or livestock was to be auctioned. That responsibility would fall to Mr. Moon as executor. I assume any

97

inventory of said effects is in his possession.'

'What would you estimate Mr. Claude-better's personal worth was?'

'Oh, it was low seven figures. Not what it had been when he first moved here, but still quite substantial.'

'He was worth less now than when he sold his company?'

'So it seems. I don't think he was a very smart investor. He was dipping into his principal too much. But he was sufficiently wealthy not to care, it seems.'

'I've known a few wealthy folks,' Wilma ventured, 'and it always seemed to me that all they were about was protecting the money and making it grow. They struck me as not believing you could be too rich.'

'Clyde,' Stillman said wryly, 'was definitely not like most wealthy folks.'

The remainder of the conversation did not yield any useful information, unless Wilma had had interest in learning more Latin phrases. Feeling some urgency to return to the station and deal with the unwelcome press conference, she soon thanked Stillman, participated in a few more short niceties, and excused herself to get back to the office.

One thought did cross her mind as she departed: was it Clyde who was spending down the worth of the estate, or was it his administrator, Marlowe Moon?

4

Wilma returned to the station to find that Natalie had things well under control. The multi-purpose area that served as briefing room and conference chamber had been set up with folding chairs and a podium. Natalie and a deputy were stationed like ushers to route everyone into seats. The two local TV stations and the Nightingale *Tribune* were represented, along with a local giveaway paper, Wilma noted with some amusement. There were already camera operators setting up. She got the briefing underway only ten minutes behind schedule and kept it short and simple, laying out what bare facts there were about the death of Clyde Claudebetter, stressing that the investigation had only just begun and that her department was devoting its full energies to uncovering the facts and finding the person or persons responsible. Holly Travers had a question before

Wilma could finish her final sentence.

'Chief, are you confident that your department has sufficient resources to handle this kind of case? Wouldn't the sheriff's department be better qualified by virtue of manpower and experience?'

Wilma maintained her impassive face but paused for a few moments before answering. 'Ms. Travers, as I told you, this is a jurisdictional matter and the sheriff's department has duly deferred to us. I would point out to you that both our department and theirs work with the same county resources, the crime lab and the coroner's office, and there's little if any difference in how the case would be handled, whoever had the jurisdiction.'

'But the sheriff's department has five full-time detectives, whereas your department has none. Are you certain you're up to this kind of high-profile challenge?' The room grew noticeably quieter.

Wilma remembered facing down two really big bikers in a bar a few years ago who were approaching her with pool cues and sneers. She was scared and really angry, but she just smiled sweetly at both of the boys, knowing that just outside the door of the bar, three equally burly deputies were about to enter. Now, she kept her body language neutral and assumed the exact same beatific smile. The police personnel in the room silently traded looks; they knew that expression and it usually meant it was a good time to get out of the Chief's way.

'I have full confidence in this department,' Wilma said in measured tones, 'and so should you, Ms. Travers, I assure you.'

Wilma fielded a few routine questions to clarify the scant information she had provided and then she ended the conference, promising to furnish updates as they became available. Two deputies shepherded the news people out of the room. Wilma walked down the short corridor to her office and plopped herself in her chair behind her desk, exhaling loudly.

'Well, at least that was short and sweet. Seemed to go all right, don't you think?'

Natalie, who had followed her, stood in the doorway. 'You did good, Chief.'

'Wish I felt as confident about all this as I tried to sound. By the way, nice job handling all that.'

'Thanks. What next?'

'I'll let you know as I figure it out. Right now I need to do some thinking. Do me a favor and ask reception to hold any calls for a while, okay?'

'You got it.'

The communications officer was barely out the door when Wilma's cell phone started vibrating in her pocket. So much for a few moments to get her thoughts together.

'This is Chief Acosta.'

'Chief, this is Marlowe Moon.' His voice was agitated, almost breaking. 'I've just completed a quick inventory of the memorabilia room, and there does seem to be something missing.'

'All right, Mr. Moon, calm down now. What's missing?'

'The Curtis Cray guitar!'

'Excuse me?'

'Curtis Cray! The rockabilly musician?'

'Okay. And his guitar, you say, is missing?'

Moon sighed impatiently. It was clear to him she wasn't getting the import here. 'Curtis Cray was an esteemed pioneer in his genre of music in the 50s and 60s. He and Mr. Claudebetter were great friends years ago. Before he died, Cray gave him one of his first electric guitars, an early model solid-body Fender Telecaster. It's worth a fortune.'

'And it was in Mr. Claudebetter's collection, and now you say it's gone?'

'Yes! Yes! It was in a square padded case on a shelf. There's a big empty spot where it used to sit.'

'All right, listen to me, Mr. Moon. Have the lab techs left?'

'No. They were still packing up. I ran down and got them and they're going to process the room.'

Good for Rosie. 'Have you touched much since you entered the room?'

'Not really. The techs came back with me making sure I didn't. Most everything is out in the open, so I didn't touch or move anything.'

'That sounds good, Mr. Moon. Thank you for your cooperation. And have you heard from Alia the housekeeper yet?'

'As a matter of fact, I did. She sounds terrible. She said she caught the flu and wanted to stay home, but I prevailed upon her against my better judgment to come in around two o'clock to speak with you. She'll likely infect us all with her germs.'

'Thank you for that as well. I'll be at the house at two.'

'Better bring a lot of hand sanitizer,' he said and hung up.

* * *

Alia Mulier had already arrived and was sitting in the same parlor where Wilma had earlier interviewed the other house-keepers. She was seated in a far corner — Moon had likely quarantined her to a remote sector — holding a tissue to her nose. She had brown hair that was covered by a knit hat and wore large dark glasses, but despite her disheveled appearance, she had gone to the trouble to apply dark lipstick. She started to rise as Moon escorted Wilma into the room,

105

but Wilma waved her back down.

'No need to get up for me, Ms. Mulier. Thank you for coming. I'm sorry you're not feeling well.'

Moon found a chair as far away from the housekeeper as possible. Wilma took a seat between them. Germs didn't tend to scare her; she had a notoriously strong constitution and hadn't taken a sick day in years. She already had her ever-present notebook in hand.

'I'm sorry I feel so miserable, Chief. I do want to help. This is horrible, what's happened to Mr. Claudebetter.' Her voice was a hoarse whisper. Wilma leaned in to hear better. 'This flu or whatever, it seems to have just come over me. I was feeling a little off yesterday afternoon but I figured it would just pass.'

Moon did not look pleased at this revelation that a sick woman might have been touching surfaces all over the house. Wilma wondered if he would be calling the county disease control center after she left.

'So you're the evening housekeeper here, I am told?'

'Yes. I've been working here about, oh, four or five weeks now. I work three to seven Monday to Friday.'

'So tell me about yesterday. You worked your regular shift and left at seven?'

'Yes. By the end of the day I wasn't feeling well at all, so I left a little early. I'm sorry, Mr. Moon; I forgot to sign out.'

Moon simply crossed his arms and glowered.

'Did you see Mr. Claudebetter at all yesterday?'

'He was in the house most of the afternoon. He said hello but otherwise we didn't speak.'

'Is that unusual?'

She coughed, holding the tissue to her mouth. 'No. Sometimes he'd ask me to take care of something, like to clean up or pay particular attention to something, but generally I get my instructions from Mr. Moon. I didn't usually talk with Mr. Claudebetter. Oh my God, this is so awful.'

'Ms. Mulier, did you happen to go down to the garage or the apartment yesterday?'

'Yes. Towels and linens are changed every week whether or not they've been used. Usually the old ones are put in the laundry, but the washing machine down there isn't working right now, so they were washed and dried in the laundry up here in the house. I brought freshly cleaned towels down to the apartment.'

'Did you drive them down there?'

'No. It was a nice day, and it's not a very long walk, so I carried them down.'

'In a laundry basket?'

'Yes, that's right.'

'And you replaced the towels and brought the old ones back up to the house?'

Mulier bit her lip and paused. 'No. To be honest, I began to realize at that point I really wasn't feeling very well, so I stored the fresh towels in the linen closet and figured I'd come back the next day and change out the towels. Nobody was staying there, and I thought it wouldn't matter if they waited a day. I just walked back to the house. It was getting late in the day by then.' She stopped as if unsure if she should continue. 'By the time I returned up the hill, I really wasn't well. In fact I . . . well, I threw up when I got back to the house.'

Wilma shot a sideways glance at Moon, who looked as if he was going into shock.

'I'm sorry, Mr. Moon,' Mulier said quietly. 'Anyway, it was near the end of my shift, so I cleaned things up and left. I suppose I wasn't really paying attention and forgot to sign out.'

'I hope you used the antibiotic soap,' Moon muttered.

Wilma ignored him. 'So you were down at the apartment about what time, would you say?'

'A little past six.'

'Was anyone else there when you were?'

'No. It was empty. There was just me.'

'You didn't see Mr. Claudebetter around there, in the garage or the apartment?'

'No. I didn't see him at all, there or back at the house.' She coughed again. At this point, Wilma wondered if Moon would have a conniption coming on.

'So you were in the garage and the apartment, is that correct?'

'No. I didn't go into the garage. Just the apartment. The washing machine is off the garage, but as I said, there was no reason for me to go there since the machine's broken.'

'But you left the laundry basket there, is that correct?'

'Yes. I left it in the upstairs hallway near the linen closet. I planned to fill it when I returned the next day and bring it back here.'

Wilma looked at the notes she had been jotting. Her notebook hadn't seen this much work in ages. 'Do I have this right, then? You entered the apartment around six p.m. and were the only person there. You left shortly thereafter, returned to the house, and to your knowledge nobody else was in the garage or the apartment?'

'The garage seemed locked up,' Mulier said, 'but I didn't try the doors and didn't look inside. To the best of my knowledge nobody was there, but I couldn't swear to it.'

'And you left the ranch a little before seven?'

'Yes.'

'Your car is parked up here, I assume, and you drove down to the gate and got buzzed out?'

'That's right. I park behind the house. I'd say I left about 6:45.'

'You have to contact someone to open the gate to let you out, don't you? Who did that?'

'It was Mr. Chalmers. He always says to have a pleasant night over the intercom when he opens the gate.'

'And you went right home?'

'And right to bed. As I said, by then I was really beginning to feel awful.' To punctuate the point, she pulled out a fresh tissue and sneezed into it. Moon actually stood up and moved further out of the room toward the doorway.

'All right, Ms. Mulier, I've got your phone number and address from Mr. Moon and I'll be in touch if I have any further questions. I appreciate your coming in to talk to me. Please call me if you can think of anything that might help.' She had a business card at the ready and stood up, leaning over to hand it to her. Mulier hesitated, put the tissues in her lap, and reached out with two hands to take the card by the edges. Wilma watched her trembling fingers as she took it. This was one sick woman. But she had, Wilma noted, gone to the trouble to tend to her nails: they were short, recently trimmed, and a glossy deep magenta. It matched her dark lipstick, which she had also gone to the trouble to apply before coming over. Well, that was how some people dealt with being sick: taking care of little grooming things might lift their spirits. Still, it was an incongruous minor element that only made her seem stranger.

Mulier nodded and stood up, tucking the card and her tissues into the pocket of her coat. 'I feel so terrible about all of this,' she rasped. 'Mr. Moon, I'm sorry I can't be here to help for a day or two. I'll try to feel better; I know you're going to need all of us.'

Moon was trying to look stoic. 'Not at all. Take as much time as you need to feel better. It's going to be chaos around here for a day or two anyway.'

Wilma waited in the parlor while Moon trailed Mulier to the door, keeping his distance from her. When he returned, he had a dispenser of sanitizing wipes and a can of disinfectant spray.

'Oh my God,' he muttered as he wiped and sprayed. 'I hope that was worth it.'

Wilma watched him with some amusement while she tried to pin down what, exactly, was bothering her the most about the interview she had just concluded with the strange young woman.

★ ★ ★

There was no peace back in her office; almost immediately her desk phone began ringing.

'Wilma, it's Will Marshall. I just finished the autopsy and I'm sending over the results, but thought I'd give you the basic overview right away.'

'Appreciate that, Will. I'll give Natalie a heads-up to expect your email. I'm still not real good at that stuff.'

'I'm afraid I don't have all that much to pass on. It's pretty much as I sized it up at the scene. He was hit hard around his left temple, apparently by a rounded corner of something large and square. That in itself might not have killed him, but when he fell, his head met that concrete floor hard. I'd say that impact was the actual cause of death.'

'Large and square. So we're talking, like, a hammer or a club?'

'I can't rule it out, but I'd say no. Last time I saw anything similar to this was when an old lady fell and struck her head on the edge of a display case at the county museum a few years back. It's like a blunt corner of some kind.'

'Will, are you saying it's possible he fell and hit his head on, say, a table or a display case, and was moved to the garage afterward?'

'That wouldn't be consistent with the evidence. He died where he stood — or rather, where he fell, right there.'

'So he was hit with something hard and square, like it was swung at him?'

'That's correct. The angle of the blow was up from below the point of impact. It wasn't brought down on his head from above. I'd say you're looking for someone his height or slightly shorter, who swung something up at the side of his head.'

Wilma chewed that over for a moment. 'How tall was Clyde?'

'I've got it here in my notes. Five-eleven. Not all that tall a man.'

'You seem sure the attacker wasn't taller than Clyde, but whatever the weapon was, why couldn't a taller person have hit him with an uppercut?'

'Gut feeling. The angle would have been awkward for that kind of a swing. I'm not saying it *couldn't* have happened that way, but all my experience tells me no.'

'All those cars in there, not a lot of room to swing something big.'

'Maybe a car had been moved out. I can't speak to that part, of course. That's your job.'

Wilma sighed heavily. 'Thanks to Dal Nickerson.'

'Yeah, well, you and I both know Dal's not a great sheriff. But I didn't say that, and if you quote me I'll deny it on a stack of bibles.'

'Didn't hear a word, Will. But I guess I agree.'

'The county board of supervisors has been pressuring him to trim his expenses, and the last thing they want is an expensive investigation. He's not great under fire, and right now between his budget cuts and that turf war, he's downright gun-shy. Between you and me, I don't think he would have done as good a job as you're going to do, even with his bigger resources.'

'Thanks for the vote of confidence. I wish I felt anywhere near as confident.'

When Will had rung off, she got up, grabbed a pile of papers, and headed off to Natalie's office down the hall. The young woman looked up from her computer and smiled.

'Natalie, I hate to do this to you, but do you mind putting in a little extra time tonight?'

'Not at all, Chief. I sort of figured you might need all hands on deck to deal with this.'

'The coroner's office is sending through the autopsy results on Mr Claudebetter, and I'm hoping there'll be at least preliminary results from the crime lab. Can you organize that and print it all out for me?'

'You got it.'

'And I'm wondering if you could do some internet searching for me. Whatever you can find on these employees of Mr. Claudebetter.' She handed Natalie the data, which included Chalmers, Moon and Bivins, that she had received from Moon. 'This is everything I know about them right now. I'd like to know more.'

Natalie gave the sheets a once-over. 'No problem.'

'I'd also like you to look into a Stanley Parker, son of a Bonnie Claudebetter Parker. I'm guessing date of birth about 35 years ago in Tennessee. Maybe make that window about 30 to 40 years or so. Sorry to be so vague on the age.'

Natalie jotted down the information. 'Sure. If there's any record out there, I'll find it.'

'Also, could you do a search on a Stacy or Stephanie Parker, same mother? Maybe expand the window further. Might be a younger sibling.'

'Got it. Anything else?' Wilma could tell her adjutant was really in her element now and eager to jump in. She still felt bad about asking her to stay late.

'I hope this isn't taking you away from anything, like that boyfriend of yours.'

Natalie made a wry face. 'Right now, uh-uh. I just gave him the boot. Nothing much waiting for me after work for the moment.'

'Oh, I'm sorry, Nat.' Actually Wilma had had some misgivings about the guy from the few times she'd met him, but had never felt comfortable saying anything.

'Don't be. It's all for the best. Next guy I find isn't going to be quite so fond of waitresses and roadhouses. Anyway, go have yourself a good evening, Chief, and don't worry about me. I'm going to have some fun chasing down these rabbits tonight.'

* * *

Wilma came home to find George sitting on the couch strumming his old Martin

118

guitar. He looked up as she entered their living room and flopped down on a chair next to him.

'Hey, darlin'. Got a pot roast that's been simmerin' in the slow cooker. Dinner's ready whenever you are.'

'Best news I've had all day. Never really got lunch.'

'That's me, slaving over a hot stove all day for ya.' Since retiring from the Amberville police department, George had been happy to be a homebody. He spent most days tinkering in his garage workshop or reading or watching television, but he always made sure to have dinner on the table when Wilma came home. There would be a discussion of her day, and he was never hesitant to contribute the benefit of his wisdom and experience. Wilma often found it best to silently tolerate this wisdom.

'What's with the guitar, George? You haven't had that thing out in years.'

'Yeah, well, my old friend Lawrence came through town today with his guitar so I dragged this out to play with him. I'm not half as rusty as I feared.' He hit a few slightly off-key chords. Wilma suppressed a wince.

George stopped playing and set his guitar down next to him on the sofa. 'But how was your day?'

'Oh, Lord, you must have heard about Clyde Claudebetter, didn't you?'

'The reclusive Tennessee Pieman himself? No. Haven't heard a thing about him in years, and I haven't turned on the TV all day. What about him?'

'He got himself killed up on his ranch. And it's my case.'

'What? How'd that happen?'

'Dal Nickerson shuffled it off on me. Seems the property had a new addition that's in Amberville proper. And I'm sick of explaining it to everybody.'

'Dal did that to you, did he? That weasel. Never did trust him. Think he's still sore at you for winning the cookoff last year?'

'I would hope he's not that petty. Will Marshall told me that Dal had a major jurisdictional battle recently and he's still gun-shy. Who knows? He was within his rights to pass the case to me. Anyway, I

got this major murder dropped in my lap.'
She stood up. 'But I'm hungry and you
say there's a pot roast waiting, so let's talk
about it over dinner.'

★ ★ ★

'So,' said George through a mouthful of
carrots and potatoes, 'you've got yourself
one hell of a murder investigation.'

'I swear, George, it's like something out
of one of those crime shows you like to
watch. I really feel I'm in over my head.
I'm not like that old lady detective that
used to be your favorite.'

'That's fiction. Real life isn't like that,
Wilma, you and I both know that.'

'But it *is* like that. It's just like that! He
was killed in a locked garage. I've got this
cast of suspects with funny names and
they're all pretty much crazy people.'

'Hold on, maybe you should start at
the beginning here.'

George could be a trial, but Wilma
often found it beneficial to organize her
thoughts by telling him everything about
some problem or issue at work. This time

it took longer to put a timeline together for him, but it definitely helped her to build a better perspective for herself. Her story and the pot roast were finished at the same time.

George finished the last few scraps on his plate and said, 'That's downright surreal. I can't remember anything like that ever happening in Amberville. And you're right, that cast sounds right out of Hollywood. So you've got a prissy little guy named Marlowe Moon . . . '

'He's a fussy one, all right.'

'Gotta wonder how a guy like that wound up working for the Tennessee Pieman. And then there's that Purvis Chalmers guy, who sounds like something out of the Grand Ole Opry show.'

'He's a likable fellow, but he's laying on the country pretty thick. He's clearly pretty sharp under that act too. He's either trying to tell me something, subtle-like, or trying to hide something from me, and I'm not sure which just yet.'

'And then you got that weird little chauffeur fellow. What's his name, Bekins?'

'Roy Bivins. Middle initial G.'

George started laughing.

'What?'

'Remember back in school how we remembered the colors of the rainbow? Roy G Biv! Red, orange, yellow, green, blue . . .'

'Indigo, violet,' Wilma finished.

'Your chauffeur's a colorful sort!'

Wilma frowned. 'Seems like there are a few people involved in this who have reason to hate their parents for what they got named. Bonnie and Clyde and now Roy G. Biv . . . ins.'

George raised his eyebrows. 'Maybe it's not his real name?'

'Maybe not, George. I'll have to wait and see what Natalie can dig up on him.'

'And then you got this mysterious afternoon maid . . .'

'Housekeeper, please.'

'Housekeeper, then. What's her name, Alia?'

'Alia Mulier. They all sound like characters out of a book or TV show, don't they?'

'As I said, this isn't fiction though,

Wilma.' George paused, looking down at his hands on the table. 'But if it were . . . '

'If it were, what?'

He peered up at her from under a raised eyebrow. 'If it were a TV show . . . I'd think they were *all* assumed names and *everybody* had something to hide.'

Wilma stood up and picked up their plates. 'I wish this *was* a TV show. I could call on one of those super-smart detectives. I wish I could at least call in that real detective from down in the city, Frank What's-his-name, who came through here a while ago.'

'As I recall, he wouldn't have broken his case without your help. You'll handle this just fine, Wilma. I know you. You're the smartest woman in the county and beyond. And maybe the *second* smartest law enforcement agent.'

'You being the first, of course,' Wilma snorted. 'Hand me your fork.'

She brought the dishes to the kitchen sink and headed back for more of the plates, shaking her head. One of these days George would get it in his head to help clear the table. Or not.

'So you and Lawrence got together today. How is he?'

'Seems good. We didn't talk all that much, mostly played. Well, I listened as much as I played, but it was fun. Lots of the old tunes we used to play together.'

'Isn't he living in Sacramento or Reno or somewhere like that?'

'Sacramento. He's had opportunity to play a lot in a band, so his playing is really good. He does a lot of acoustic fingerpicking. He even grew his nails, just on his right hand, so he can pluck the strings and get the right sound.'

'Now, that's interesting. So he's got long nails on his right hand but not his left?'

'Yeah, he keeps the nails on his left hand clipped short so he can fret the notes and chords.' He gazed down at his own fingers and wiggled them like a kid playing an air guitar. 'He sure does some nice fingerpicking. Maybe I should try growing my nails like that; maybe I could play like him.'

'George, you haven't played that thing in years until today.'

'I know. I'm just saying. Maybe I would if I could sound like that.'

'As if it'd be that easy.' Wilma looked at her own nails. 'Grew them long on one hand, clipped them short on the other. Hmm.'

She brought more plates and glasses back to the sink, this time plunged into thought.

'I know that look,' George called from the dining room table.

'George, you can't even see my face.'

'Don't have to. I know that look so well I can feel it. I can see your shoulders and hear how silent you got. You just figured something out.'

'Maybe,' she said absently. 'Maybe.'

Her thoughts were interrupted by the buzz of her cell phone in her pocket. She wiped off her hands and pulled it out.

Marlowe Moon identified himself, sounding even more agitated than earlier. 'I'm sorry to bother you. I hope it's not too late.'

'Not a problem, Mr. Moon, if it's important.'

'Remember I told you earlier that the

Curtis Cray guitar had been stolen?'

'Yes, sir.'

'Well, it hasn't! It's still here!'

'Now, wait a minute . . . where are you, sir?'

Moon was talking at supersonic speed. It was a wonder his words stayed in line in the proper order. 'I'm still at the ranch. I plan to stay here tonight. I decided to go through the memorabilia room to see if anything else had been taken. I had a talk with Mr. Claudebetter's attorney, and he advised me to double-check the inventory of belongings. I'm beside myself with agitation right now and I can hardly think straight, so I thought I might as well occupy myself with some routine task like the inventory . . . '

'Yes, sir, I get it. And?'

'Whoever took the guitar did not get the Cray guitar, only the Cray case.'

'They took an empty case?'

'Well, no, that's not quite right. There was another guitar in it.'

'Maybe you need to back up just a little bit, Mr. Moon.'

Moon heaved a huge sigh before

continuing, trying to compose himself or express frustration with her; she didn't really care either way, as long as he slowed down.

'There's a second guitar missing from the collection. It's not as valuable. It's a cheap foreign knockoff of an expensive Fender guitar from many years ago; that was Mr. Claudebetter's first guitar from when he was learning to play. It was in a case about the same size and shape as the Cray, just a much cheaper one. He kept it solely for sentimental reasons. He even told me once that he doubted it was playable any more, something about the neck being warped. But looking over my master list, I noted that it was also missing. I couldn't imagine anyone stealing it with so much more valuable material around, so I searched all around to see if perhaps it had been misplaced elsewhere. In my searches, I happened to unlock the laundry room, and found the cheaper guitar case in there. I opened it up and . . . '

'You found the Cray guitar inside?' Wilma finished.

'Exactly.'

'And the other guitar and case are nowhere to be found?'

'That's correct.'

'So apparently someone switched guitars and cases and took the good case with the bad guitar, and hid the expensive guitar in the bad case in the laundry room?'

'Yes! It doesn't make any sense at all!'

Wilma thought for a long moment, sensing Moon's impatience at her silence. 'Is it possible that the person who stole the guitar didn't know they were getting the wrong one?'

'Oh . . . I don't know. At this point, anything's possible, I suppose! Are you suggesting that one person switched it and a different person stole it? This is crazy!'

'I don't know, but is there a place you can move that guitar and case to where it'll be safe for now?'

'Yes, of course.'

'Someplace away from the garage and the memorabilia room. Maybe up in the main house, locked up securely?'

'I can do that. But . . . '

'And, Mr. Moon, is there a way you can prevent anyone from coming onto the grounds tonight? Can you disable the gate?'

'Yes, I can. But when the security company comes through . . . '

'You can call them and tell them not to come by tonight. I'll put an officer on your gate. If nobody can get in there tonight, that'd be good.'

'You're thinking the thief might come back for the Cray guitar?'

'I don't know for sure, sir. Just a precaution. When will your employees start showing up tomorrow morning?'

'I gave everybody the day off, so likely it will just be me and Chalmers here tomorrow. We'll be starting to plan the services and so forth.'

'That's fine. I'll be by first thing in the morning and you can buzz me into the gate. Don't let anybody else in, all right?'

'Well, actually the lawyer's supposed to come by in the morning to discuss things.'

'Nate Stillman? Around what time?'

'I wanted him to come at eight, but he said he'd be here at ten.'

'I'll be there by then, so that's okay. But nobody else, understood?'

Moon sighed heavily. 'Yes, yes. I'll see you in the morning, but I doubt I'm going to get much sleep tonight. This is all driving me crazy.'

Wilma was about to dial the station and the night dispatcher when her phone buzzed again, showing the station number.

'Chief, it's Natalie. I hope I'm not calling you too late.'

'Not at all. I was about to call in. What're you still doing at work?'

'I got caught up in the stuff you asked me to do. I printed out Will Marshall's full report and Rosie Flores's preliminaries. They're on your desk for when you come in tomorrow. I also wrote up a report on what I could find on the people at the ranch, but I thought I'd tell you about it before I left for the night.'

'I appreciate that. Anything of interest?'

'Not much be found on Marlowe Moon, just a local address at the Hillman

Inn up in Buckhorn. He obtained a driver's license a few months before coming to work for Claudebetter. Everything else I find about him is since he became the principal administrator of the Claudebetter ranch. If he had a life before that, it's a mystery.'

'He submitted a résumé to work there.'

'Yes, and I've got it here, but there's no confirmation, no record of him anywhere online.'

'Birth, baptism, marriage, anything?'

'I did some searches in the national data banks without any luck. If I could narrow him down to a locale, maybe I could dig further.'

'Possibly he changed his name when he moved here.'

'That's what I was thinking, but so far I also haven't found any notice of a legal name change. I'll do some more searching tomorrow. Now, Purvis Chalmers goes way back to Nashville. Plenty on him but nothing all that unusual. Some minor scrapes with the law when he was around twenty, the usual good-old-boy stuff, drunk and disorderly. No prison record or anything like that. You'll find his history in my report.'

'Okay.'

'Now, Mr. Bivins, he's another enigma. Again, his application is un-confirmable. Absolutely no information on him whatsoever. Not even a driver's license.'

'What? How is that possible? He's a *chauffeur*, for Pete's sake! He had to have written down a license number on his application!'

'He did, but the department of motor vehicles has nothing on him. I can't find any official records for someone with that name. Not even a birth certificate.'

Wilma scratched her head. Natalie continued. 'I had the same problem with Alia Mulier. I found two people with that name; one is ninety-four and lives in Tucson; the other lived in Montreal until she passed away two years ago.'

'This is crazy, Natalie. All of those people were vetted by an employment agency. They were even fingerprinted.'

'Well, that's the crazy thing, Chief. Some of them were, and some of them weren't.'

'What's that supposed to mean?'

'There are prints in the FBI's IAFIS file for Marlowe Moon and Purvis Chalmers, as there should be for anybody fingerprinted as a background check. But there are no records of fingerprints for Roy Bivins or Alia Mulier.'

'Now that's just downright crazy.'

'The agency that did some of the background checks was noted, so I tried giving them a call. As luck would have it, they have an evening staff. The person I spoke with couldn't find an application for Bivins or Mulier. She said that they no longer work with the Claudebetter Ranch because of some kind of disagreement over payment due and haven't heard from anybody there since.'

'So maybe Marlowe Moon used some other agency for staffing since then.'

'That's what I figured. If you'd like, in the morning, I can start making calls around to all the agencies and see if I can find out where Alia Mulier's application was submitted.'

'Wait on that for now. I'll ask Moon tomorrow about that.' Wilma sighed.

'How about Stanley Parker, how'd you fare on him?'

'Got a birth certificate for Stanley Alton Parker, born thirty-nine years ago to Bonnie Claudebetter Parker, father's name Alton Parker, in Nashville, Tennessee. Apparently the only child to the mother. No other birth records, at least under the mother's name.'

'So, no births for a Stacy or a Stephanie or . . . '

'Not that I could find. But I did find a Stacy Parker who popped up in Atlanta about ten years ago. She was a professional musician who enjoyed some minor success for a few years around Houston, New Orleans, and Atlanta. Then she disappeared. I didn't find anything that would connect her to Claudebetter or Parker though. There was a bad photo on a bar poster that I found online. The scan wasn't very good, but I printed a copy of it and left it with the rest of the data on your desk. Probably a wild goose chase, though.'

'Probably. So if Stanley had a sibling . . . '

'My guess would be she's what they used to call illegitimate, from an affair or a hot fling of some kind.' Natalie started to giggle and cleared her throat. 'Sorry, Chief. I'm getting giddy from the energy drinks. What I mean is, a half-sister might exist, but she'd have a different name, maybe. She could have been given up for adoption. Lots of things could have happened.'

Wilma was reminded of the case she had helped that city detective to solve last year. It had involved a complicated adoption. It was only sheer luck that she had been able to find sufficient information to locate the person her colleague had been looking for. If there was an adopted half-sibling involved in this case, the odds were strongly against her being able to untangle the answers. It had been a long shot anyway, but the question of the mysterious Stacy or Stephanie, or whoever, was a dead end.

'And I guess that's about it. Everything's on your desk.' Wilma heard her stifle a yawn. 'Unless there's anything else, I think I'll head home now and see you in the morning.'

'Okay, thanks, Natalie. You've gone beyond the call of duty. Could I ask you to do one more thing before you leave? Who's out on patrol tonight?'

'That would be Deputies Mitchell and Perkins.'

'Both decent men. Please tell the night dispatcher to radio one of them and tell them to park themselves outside the front gate to the Claudebetter ranch and make sure nobody enters or leaves until I get there in the morning. Nobody.'

'Sure. Mitchell's closer, so I'll have her call him.'

'Perfect. Thanks again, Natalie. Get yourself some well-earned sleep, now.'

George was still sitting at the table, watching Wilma. She wearily punched off her phone and returned it to her pocket and he said, 'Is this going to be one of those things where you don't sleep all night?'

'Lord, no. You just watch. I'm going to sleep like a newborn baby.'

'Just as long as you don't snore, darlin'.

5

Wilma arrived at the station before six the next morning. Her plan was to do some prep and get to the ranch by eight. Jim Burton would be coming on, and she would have him follow her over to spell Guy Mitchell at the gate.

As Natalie had promised, a pile of papers awaited her arrival. She sat down with her coffee cup and started leafing through them. The very first sheet was a photocopy of a map of the area, with the crime scene circled in red ink. It was indeed just barely over the line and part of Amberville. There was also a note that Natalie had called the security company, and the patrol that had come through the ranch the evening of the murder had reported nothing out of the ordinary encountered during their routine spin around the garage. Her adjutant was admirably thorough.

As anticipated, there was no new

information in either the coroner's report or the preliminary crime lab findings. Clyde had been killed by a single blow to the side of the head and the resultant impact with the floor. No weapon consistent with the forensic evidence had been found. No other blood stains had been found, and there was no evidence of the body having been moved from elsewhere. There was no sign of any kind of forced entry or exit around the garage or the apartment. It was conceivable that someone had been in various parts of the apartment and the garage, but the doors had already been opened, or the persons passing through them possessed keys. Fingerprints were present in huge amounts, many smeared or overlapping; processing was ongoing and would likely take a while.

She carefully perused all of Natalie's report on her online findings regarding Clyde's employees. It was all exactly as Natalie had summarized for her the previous evening. Purvis Chalmers's life was pretty much an open book; in fact if anything, there was too much trivial information on the man, some of it slightly surprising. Marlowe Moon was easy to follow until one tried to delve back before he had showed up at the Pumpkin Ranch. And Bivins and Mulier were two total ciphers.

The information on Stanley Parker covered half a sheet of paper. The photo of the southeastern musician Stacy Parker was a bad scan of a bad photo of the poster and could have been anyone. That was clearly an irrelevant trail. There was a scarcity of any kind of information, and what was to be found seemed to have no pattern as yet.

She found herself wishing that detective Frank Vandegraf were around. On the surface, he'd seemed to be a kind of plodding sort, but she had been impressed by the intelligence and method that were hidden by that appearance. How would he handle something like this? She figured he'd make notes, assemble everything however inconsequential it seemed, then look for connections. He'd worry all the facts to death, trying to fit everything together like a tableful of pieces from a clock. She looked at the notepad on her desk and picked up a pen.

Wilma started idly jotting notes, hoping to see patterns emerging. She found herself drawing arrows between the names she had written down: Bivins, Chalmers, Mulier, Moon . . . arranged around Claudebetter in the center.

The answers had to lie in that thicket of characters. She also wrote 'Stanley?' and 'Stacy?' off to the side but found herself returning to the nucleus she had created.

She scribbled 'Guitar?' to one side as well and started drawing arrows to names and comments. Her thoughts swirled as she wrote.

Somebody was in the apartment. They wanted the guitar and stole it. Was it the same person who killed Clyde? Did Clyde show up and confront them?

A car had to have been pulled out of the garage, to leave a space large enough for the killer to be able to swing something hard enough to knock Clyde down, then returned to the garage thereafter. So somebody had the keys to the garage *and* the apartment. *And* at least one of the cars.

The killer was no taller than Clyde, according to the forensic evidence, and conceivably shorter.

The killer was likely there before Clyde arrived, and had already taken the guitar.

The guitar case was heavy and rectangular, with blunt metal corners. Consistent with the murder weapon.

Somebody had called Clyde, claiming to be a niece who didn't exist, saying she urgently needed to speak with him. Why did that seem so important?

Someone had switched guitars before they arrived and locked the Cray guitar in the laundry room. They apparently knew that someone else was coming for it.

Guitar players.

And then there was that other thing that her mind had been gnawing at like a dog with a bone last night and this morning. It defied logic. The only way she could reconcile it was almost as illogical.

That famous detective in the books and the movies had said, when you removed the impossible, whatever was left, however improbable, had to be the truth.

Wilma shook her head. It just kept feeling more and more like she was actually in one of those movies rather than real life.

★   ★   ★

When Jim Burton checked in, Wilma collared him to follow her over to the ranch. They arrived almost at eight on the dot. Guy Mitchell's cruiser was drawn up in front of the gate, alongside a nice late model Lexus, and the deputy and a man in a blue pinstripe suit were standing near the vehicles talking earnestly. They looked up as the police vehicles pulled in alongside.

'Mr. Stillman, I'm surprised to see you here this morning.'

'Yes, well, Mr. Moon seemed insistent that I see him first thing this morning, so here I am. The only problem is that Deputy Mitchell here won't let me in.'

'He's doing what I asked him to, sir. I don't see any reason you shouldn't be able to follow me in right now.' She turned to Mitchell. 'Anybody else seek entry here, Guy?'

'No, Chief; it's been quiet. Hardly even any traffic up and down the highway all night. Mr. Stillman here was my first customer, and he just got here.'

'Jim can take over for you. You can head on back and clock out.' She walked to the gate and pressed the intercom button to inform Marlowe Moon that she and Nate Stillman had arrived. In another minute, the automatic gate began to slide open.

'Jim, I need you to station yourself right here and inform me if anyone wants to enter. I believe that all the staff has been given the day off, but I don't know if anybody has business coming or going, so be sure to check with me.'

Burton nodded. Everyone headed to their vehicles. Mitchell left a trail of dust and gravel as he pulled his cruiser back onto the asphalt. Wilma followed Stillman's car into the ranch. As the gate automatically closed behind them, Jim Burton pulled his cruiser around to block the gate.

Moon was awaiting their arrival on the portico to the Claudebetter hacienda. They both pulled around the circular drive and parked.

'Mr. Stillman, this is a surprise,' Moon said, arms folded. 'Here I thought I wouldn't be seeing you for a few more hours. But I'm glad you're here.' He shifted a steely glare back and forth between the lawyer and Wilma. 'Come in, please, both of you.'

He led them to the parlor and gestured for them to sit. 'Chief, do you have any objection to Mr. Stillman sitting in on our conversation this morning?'

'Not at all, Mr. Moon, as long as you don't.'

'Well, who knows.' He smirked. 'If I'm a suspect in this tawdry affair, it might be good to have my attorney present.'

'At the moment, sir, everybody's a suspect and nobody is, if you get my meaning.'

They all deposited themselves on seats.

'I have absolutely nothing to hide, Chief, and I'm quite happy to talk to you in front of Mr. Stillman here. I had

145

nothing to do with Mr. Claudebetter's death; in fact, his passing has complicated my own life in incredibly. That's why I requested to confer with Mr. Stillman right away.'

Wilma's brain spun as she tried to decide just where to start, but she tried to maintain a cool, confident exterior. 'Just some more questions that come to mind. I assume you took care of that item we spoke about last night?'

Moon did not seem particularly concerned that Stillman was listening in. 'Yes. It's safe up here in the house, locked away.'

Wilma nodded. 'Forgive me if I jump around here. Now, tell me again about who has the keys to the apartment and the garage?'

'As I said yesterday, Mr. Claudebetter and Mr. Chalmers had keys to both. There's a set of keys to the apartment here at the main house, but the housekeepers are required to inform me if they use them.'

'If you don't happen to be immediately available, how do they do that exactly?'

'They can sign the key out and back in. There's a clipboard on the wall next to the keys.'

'That's the first I've heard of this. Were they signed out on the day Mr. Claudebetter was murdered?'

'No, they weren't. If the housekeeper, what's her name, used the keys, she never signed out or told me.'

'Ms. Mulier, you mean.'

Moon waved a hand. 'Yes, of course. She's still fairly new.'

'She's been in the employ of the ranch for a little over a month now, is that correct? Alia Mulier, I mean, whose name you still have trouble remembering.'

'Yes, yes. You have to understand, I have limited contact with the housekeeping staff. Their duties are generally clear-cut, and they go their way while I'm very occupied with affairs of the property.' It seemed to pain him to even consider having actual contact with the domestic staff, as if it were beneath him. 'Alia Mulier. I'll try to remember that.'

Stillman made a slight laugh. They both turned to look at him. 'Forgive me, the old Latin scholar coming out again.'

'I'm sorry, Mr. Stillman, but I don't get that,' Wilma said.

'Remember when I explained to you that 'inter alia' means 'among other things'? In Latin, 'alia mulier' would mean 'the other woman,' or something like that.'

'Is that so? The other woman.' Wilma nodded. Stillman looked a trifle embarrassed, as if he felt he was being patronized.

'Or perhaps 'another woman,' something along those lines. Forgive me for interrupting. I suppose I can be a bit of a pedant.'

Wilma smiled. 'Not at all, sir. That's very interesting, in fact.' She turned back to Moon. 'What about the garage? Are there keys to the garage here at the house as well?'

'Not as such. The laundry room is off the garage, so there's a key to get from the apartment into the garage, but not to open the main doors accessing the vehicles. There'd be no reason for the housekeeping staff to have those. We don't keep loose copies of those keys anywhere.'

'And those large garage doors are kept locked as a rule?'

'Oh yes. The cars in there are quite valuable.'

'How about keys to the cars themselves?'

'Anyone who has the keys to the garage also has keys to the cars.'

'So who does have access to the main garage doors and the cars?'

'Well, Roy the chauffeur, of course; and Mr. Claudebetter did. Mr. Chalmers has a set. As caretaker, he has access to everything on the property.'

'As do you, I assume, Mr. Moon.'

'Actually, no. I do have keys to the apartment, but not to the garage or the cars. If I were to need access to the garage, I'd have to get the keys from one of the others.'

Wilma sat in thought for a long moment. 'So who exactly would have had key access to both the apartment and the main garage doors? The chauffeur?'

'Not Roy. He only has the keys for the

garage and cars, not to get into the apartment, not even by the access door from the garage. The only people who would have authorized access to both would be Mr. Claudebetter and Mr. Chalmers.'

'Access seems to have been kept close to the vest around here.'

'I insisted upon that. Mr. Claudebetter chose to lead a private life here. He only wanted a handful of people working here — in recent days, economics dictated we cut back even more — and wanted to keep everyone's duties separated to the fullest extent possible.'

Wilma had to wonder how much of this was Clyde's desire and how much was Moon's.

'So the stablemen, say, would have had no access to that building.'

'Nor to this one. They come in the morning, attend to the horses and the stables, and leave in the evening. We never see them unless there's something out of the routine. Same for the gardeners.'

'Only a handful of people working here, kind of multitasking, in a pretty cloistered environment. And yet there's a full-time chauffeur. Is there really call for his services to that extent?'

Moon sighed. 'Mr. Claudebetter insisted on having Roy full-time. It was a mystery to me as well. Perhaps he had it in his mind that he might decide to start discreet trips into town again, like he used to; but I used Roy's services as a driver more than he did. He was also obsessed with keeping his collection of automobiles maintained in perfect running order. He didn't trust local mechanics, so it was Roy's job keeping them in perfect condition. Even as activities were scaled back, Mr. Claudebetter wanted to keep Roy on and would find duties for him. He seemed to hold some affinity for him on some level. It wasn't uncommon for him to ask Roy to drive to town for groceries or other basics for the ranch. He was kept busy, believe me.'

'Clyde loved his cars and his guitars.'

'Yes, I would say so.' Moon stared blankly at Wilma, as if waiting to see if she was finished with her interrogation. But she was only getting started.

'You said Mr. Claudebetter *used* to travel to town and back a lot. That had changed in recent times?'

'Over the past year especially, he increasingly kept his own counsel. He only spoke with any of us briefly. I think there was a physical problem that was beginning to bother him.'

'A physical problem? What, exactly? I heard his health was fine.'

'I think his sight and hearing were beginning to deteriorate. There were subtle signs of miscommunication that were growing.'

'Did Mr. Claudebetter seek medical attention for any of this?'

'No. He refused to acknowledge there was a problem. He hated doctors. He refused to visit one. I don't think in the whole time I worked for him that he ever had an exam or a medical visit.'

'How did he occupy his time here at the ranch?'

'He spent a lot of time with his horses. He'd play music. He'd spend time with his memorabilia. He'd grown averse to baking, especially pies, but he still liked cooking. Some of the time the housekeepers would cook, but he also wanted to do it.'

'Mr. Moon, forgive me, but it seems to me that even though you've got a small staff here, there didn't seem to be all that much for any of them to do.'

'That was one reason we cut back on staff and hours over the past year. That and economics.'

'And what, specifically, have your own duties been around here since you were hired?'

'Administration,' Moon said coolly. 'The running of the property and Mr. Claudebetter's businesses and trusts require full-time oversight.'

'Can you be more specific? My understanding is that he was retired and disenchanted with dealmakers. It doesn't sound like he did all that much business around here.'

'Mr. Claudebetter's entire source of income was the investments he had set up after he was bought out. In recent years they were somewhat volatile and needed to be managed carefully. And this is a large property. There has always been a lot to keep an eye on.'

'Sounds as if you were in need of the services of an accountant, and maybe a lawyer. Has Mr. Stillman here provided you his services, or have you brought in an accountant?'

'Not necessary. I have accounting expertise, and I'm also quite competent to handle all the pressing business matters. But they've required my constant attention on a day-to-day basis.'

'That brings me to another question, Mr. Moon. What exactly is your background? It would seem that your own personal history just comes to a dead stop going back to about the exact time you began to work for Mr. Claudebetter.'

'I provided you with a copy of the same resume I provided when I applied to work here.'

'Yes, and, well, none of it pans out, sir. Frankly, I'm not sure how you passed muster. There's no record of a Marlowe Moon anywhere before you came to the ranch. You're quite the mystery man.

Why, I can't even tell for sure where you were the other night after you left this property. I'm sure you understand how that must to look to me, and why I might find cause to look at you with a bit of suspicion?'

'I didn't kill Mr. Claudebetter. I've done nothing in the least irregular around here.'

'You need to answer the questions, then! Convince me!'

The conversation stopped dead for several beats, Wilma and Moon holding each other in stares. The only sound was Stillman, shifting uncomfortably in his seat. Finally Moon turned to the attorney.

'Mr. Stillman, would you be willing to confer with me in my office back there for a moment?'

'Why ... sure, of course,' Stillman answered in surprise.

'Chief, would you excuse us for just a few minutes?'

Wilma nodded, taken aback. The two men rose and walked to a room off of the parlor, and closed the door behind them. She sat, staring at the ceiling and around the room. The muffled voices went back and forth for some time before the door reopened and they both returned to their seats with serious expressions. Wilma raised her eyebrows expectantly, looking back and forth between them.

'Mr. Moon has requested my services as legal counsel,' Stillman said, 'and I've agreed. As per my advice, he wishes to make a statement at this time.'

Wilma turned back to Moon, a bit impatient with the jargon. 'Well, then go ahead, if you please.'

Moon cleared his throat and sniffed. 'I would not and could not have killed Mr. Claudebetter, because he was the only person I truly trusted. He was the only one who knew the truth about me and, despite that, employed and unrelentingly supported me.'

Moon hesitated and looked to Stillman, who nodded in encouragement.

'I changed my name when I moved here to work for Mr. Claudebetter because my reputation was such that I had become unemployable in my profession. I was an entertainment business manager and accountant with high-profile clients. I ran in high company . . . before I made a series of, well, bad decisions. You've perhaps heard the show business cliché 'you'll never work in this town again'? Well, that's precisely what happened to me.'

'Mr. Moon would like to stress,' Stillman interjected, 'that there were never any criminal proceedings brought against him, nor has he ever been sought, nor indicted, by any law enforcement agency in this country or elsewhere.'

'That's right. I'm not a fugitive. What I am is perhaps worse. I'm a pariah. There are threats on my person, and I wouldn't be surprised if my very life could be at stake from certain quarters. The people who employed me are powerful, and they don't play gently. Mostly they seemed to be satisfied with my disappearance from the scene as long as I didn't surface anywhere to their attention.'

'So you're saying you stole from the wrong people, Mr. Moon?' asked Wilma. 'Unsavory sorts, shall we say?'

This was clearly difficult for Moon to

discuss. He twitched and sighed. 'Among other things, yes.'

'Sounds like you were stupid, or at least pretty rash. You don't strike me as a stupid man.'

'The high life, Chief Acosta. Too many temptations. There are substances that are easy to fall in love with. And then the stupidity begins.'

Wilma nodded. The sniffles, of course. Fuentes's comment. 'Cocaine. You got strung out?'

Moon kept his eye steadily on Stillman as he continued, looking for any warning, walking a delicate line between clearing himself of suspicion of murder and incriminating himself in other crimes in the process. 'All I wish to say is that I made a series of very, very bad decisions where I formerly resided. I was looking for a fresh new start. It came to my attention that Clyde Claudebetter had put out the word he was relocating and needed a good solid all around manager.'

'How exactly did that come to your attention? Did you know Mr. Claudebetter?'

'At that point, no. I was in . . . well, let's just say I was in an urban area on the eastern seaboard. We had friends of friends. Three degrees of separation and all that. He knew a lot of musicians. A lot of musicians patronized some of the same business associates as I did.'

'You shared a drug dealer. Okay.' Wilma raised her hands. 'Mr. Moon, this all strikes me as something outside my sphere of interest, if you will. I'm only interested in what relates to the death of Clyde Claudebetter.' She looked at Stillman. 'Your lawyer here is a witness. I'm not here to entrap you for things you might have done before you came here, so long as you didn't murder or kidnap anyone or like that.'

'I've never committed a violent crime in my life,' Moon said earnestly.

'Then I think you don't need to worry if you can explain things to me, okay? I need to understand what's been going on here.'

'When I met with Mr. Claudebetter, at first I tried to act under my new identity and tell him nothing of my past. I was hoping I could convince him of my capability of running every aspect of his business and property. It was all experience and a set of skills I possessed. I knew it would be easy for me. I knew all about contracts and keeping books and so forth. The world in which I ran was full of schemes and loopholes and back-dealing. Running a straightforward business for someone like him would be like a college professor teaching kindergarten.' Moon sighed deeply.

'The interview didn't go that way. He was much smarter than that. At one point he interrupted me and said, 'Son, I can tell when a man is intelligent, and you are that, and I can tell when a man is lying, and you are also that. We can end this right now or you can start telling me the truth, and you can trust that I'll judge you on where I think you're going to go and not where you've been.' Nobody had ever talked to me like that before. I decided I'd take the chance, and I came clean to him. Then I stood up and said, 'Thank you for the interview, and I understand I'm probably not what you're looking for.' And he told me to sit back down.

' "This will all be between you and me so long as you never disappoint me,' he said; and he had me create a resume that was plausible but mostly fictional. He was surprisingly good at devising an illusionary background for me. Here I thought I would be dealing with an ingenuous rube, and instead he had as much craft and guile as any of the characters I'd ever worked with. I'd already obtained identification under my new identity, but he actually helped me solidify it in some ways. He had me fill out an employment application and file it here as if I'd applied for the job through normal channels. He even helped me establish credit. Luckily I'd never run afoul of the law and never been fingerprinted, so he had me bold-facedly march into the Nightingale police office and request to be fingerprinted for my employment records.'

'Did anybody else know about any of this?'

'No. Neither of us ever told anyone else. Not even his best friend, Purvis Chalmers, knew.'

'Mr. Chalmers doesn't seem to have exactly warmed to you over the time you've both been here.'

'He's always regarded me with suspicion. I don't blame him. To be honest, I feel the same about him. Something about that aw-shucks country-boy act. He's smarter than he lets on.'

Wilma let that slide by, even though she agreed with his assessment. 'So you've been Mr. Claudebetter's right-hand man ever since.'

'That's right. I've been the ranch major domo, so to speak, since its inception. I've built and stewarded it every step of the way.'

'I want to come back to that shortly. But first, if you really want to clear yourself of suspicion, there's another question that still has to be answered: where were you the other night after you left here?'

'I was at a meeting, Chief. My recovery group. We meet two evenings a week.'

'That substance thing you were talking about?'

Moon nodded.

'How long has it been since you stopped?'

Moon nervously looked to Stillman, who gave him a slight nod.

'I'm afraid I've had a few backslides over the years. This time it's been a few weeks . . . '

'Perhaps it's better to leave it at that,' Stillman said quickly. 'Chief, for the most part of his time here, he's been clean and sober and a loyal servant, if you will. If need be, he can substantiate his whereabouts the night of the murder, understanding a certain amount of discretion to be observed regarding his recovery group. That's the only extent to which I can countenance any further detail.'

Wilma found herself wishing he would lapse back into Latin, which she would have found less annoying than his use of English. Certain things did seem to be falling into place for her, however: Moon's fussy overanxious behavior, his incessant sniffling, the rumors that the ranch was losing money, and the resultant staff and budget cuts. The apparent inattention to details of ranch business. Moon hadn't been on the wagon several weeks. He was just trying, desperately, to scramble back on in recent days.

'Mr. Moon, I'm not interested in causing you any trouble because of any problems you might have with any substances. Your responsibilities regarding that — well, there are other people you'll have to deal with. My only concern here and now is what relates to Mr. Claudebetter's death. If there were certain things that might have been getting by you in recent days, it's important that I know, do you understand?'

'What kinds of things do you mean might have 'gotten by' me, exactly?'

'There doesn't seem to be any background information on Alia Mulier. She filled out an employment application, but nothing seems to check out. She has no official history that can be found.'

'That's news to me, Chief.' Moon looked a trifle sheepish as he said it.

'And the same thing is true of Roy Bivins. He provided you with supposed background information, but was any of it ever verified?'

'Well . . . of course.'

'Mr. Moon, we can't corroborate *anything* that either of those people said on their applications. If law enforcement can't, how did you? Do you have any records of official verification?'

Moon buried his face in his hands for several seconds before answering. 'No. No, I don't.'

'In short, there are a number of people who have been working here that you don't really know anything about for sure, am I right?'

'I've — I've always carried out my duties here to the best of my ability.'

'Mr. Moon, this isn't about you right now. This is about Roy Bivins and Alia Mulier. It's very possible that one of them is not who they claim they are, isn't it? Those applications, they were never vetted properly, were they?'

Moon's silence confirmed what she suspected. Finally he muttered quietly,

'They weren't important positions. I just kept putting it off . . . '

'I gather you haven't ever spent much time with Mr. Bivins or Miss Mulier, and you don't know much about them from personal contact.'

'I'm . . . I'm a busy man here. Running this place takes up my time.'

'I think we both know what's taking up much of your time and your attention around here. My point is that there's not much you can tell me about either of them.'

'I'm probably not what you'd consider a people person, Chief Acosta. I don't waste time on small talk with the help. My sole concern has always been that they were trustworthy and did their jobs.'

'Did you ever happen to notice if Mr. Bivins played a musical instrument or showed any interest in music?'

'How would I know? As I said, their personal lives were none of my concern.'

'But you never saw him playing, say, a guitar around here? Or talking to Mr. Claudebetter about music?'

'No, I can't say as I did.'

'Same for Miss Mulier?'

'I know nothing about either one of them beyond how they do their jobs. On that score, they both seemed to be satisfactory. Well, except for the house-keeper coming to work diseased.'

Moon, clearly uncomfortable and on the defensive, seemed unable to stop fidgeting with his hands. He reminded Wilma of people she had known who had just given up smoking. She guessed one dependency might not be all that dissimilar from another. It was making her uneasy as well. She was quite relieved to finally end the interview and excuse herself.

★ ★ ★

Wilma sat in her vehicle, thumbing the button on the communicator, sorting through the pages on the seat beside her. She found what she was looking for just as she got hold of Clarence White.

'Yes, Chief, what's up?'

'Clarence, can you make a run into

Nightingale to check on something for me?'

'Not a problem.'

She read off two addresses. 'Just drive by both of those, if you would. Keep your eyes open, see what you see. No need to stop or engage anyone on the premises. Then get back to me, okay?'

'Sure thing, Chief.' He repeated the two addresses back to her and they signed off.

Wilma put the sheets down and plucked her legal pad off the seat. She rested it on the steering wheel and, pulling out her pen, began to jot some more notes down while she waited.

It was less than twenty minutes before Clarence was back on the two-way. 'The first address checks out, but that second one . . .'

'Yes?'

'It's around the corner from the first, and there are a couple apartments upstairs, but it's mostly taken up by a business called Ship and Receive, one of those things where you can mail out packages by way of a couple of different delivery services that contract with them.'

'Is that so?'

'They also have mailboxes that can be rented.'

'That's very interesting. Thanks, Clarence. One more thing I need you to do. Give a call over to the Nightingale police, just as a courtesy, and let them know you're just taking care of something routine. And then keep an eye on that first address for me . . . '

★ ★ ★

Purvis Chalmers opened his door with an easy smile. 'Chief Acosta, nice to see you again. I don't suppose you're back for more of my coffee.'

'No, sir. Just some more questions, if you have a minute.'

'Dang, I got nothing but time right now. Come on in.' He led her into the cabin. 'So how's your investigation proceedin'? Any suspects?'

'Too many. It's a confusing case,' she said as Chalmers motioned her to a chair and sat across from her. 'I keep coming up with more questions than answers.'

'Forgive me for sayin' so,' drawled Purvis, a small smile at the corners of his mouth, 'but you seem to be actin' as if you've never had to deal with a confounding crime before.'

'No, sir,' said Wilma. 'I can't say as I've ever had one that was anything like this.'

'Surely you've seen killings. I grew up in rural Tennessee, and there were lots of 'em. Strange stuff, too. There are just as many off-kilter types in the country as in the city. Maybe more. I remember there was one individual, mutilated their victim — loppin' off fingers and toes and such — and left 'em strewed around the house.'

If he expected a shocked response from Wilma, she was going to disappoint him. She stoically smiled back at him. 'I'm no stranger to brutal violence, Mr. Chalmers. I could tell you some stories too, I'm sure. I don't know if you'd moved here yet when the sixty-five-year-old lady took an axe to her cheating boyfriend.'

Chalmers raised his eyebrows and

extended his lower lip. 'Can't say as I heard 'bout that one. Possibly before my time.'

'My point is, this is something different. Murders are most often crimes of passion. They're not particularly well thought out and they're easy to muddle through, with a little headwork and a lot of legwork. This one has a quality of purpose to it that bothers me.'

'Wonderin' if you're up to it? That'd surprise me.'

'Oh, no, I'm up to it. It's just like any other case. Keep assembling the facts and sooner or later, you see the trail.'

'So how can I help you now?'

'Are you absolutely sure Clyde didn't have a niece? Stanley couldn't possibly have had a stepsister or a half-sister or something like that?'

'Guaranteed, nope.'

'How can you be so sure? Maybe there was a relationship that Bonnie had that she wasn't particularly proud of, shall we say?'

'You're suggestin' she might have had a child by another man, someone she hid away? You're on a wild goose chase, Chief.'

'Somebody tried to contact Clyde a while ago. She claimed to be Clyde's niece and told Marlowe Moon that her name was Stephanie or Stacy or something like that. She made it seem important enough that Mr. Moon remembered it. I think it's possible she continued to try to get through to Clyde.'

Chalmers's smile had faded; his face was impassive. He leaned back in his chair, arms folded like a wall. 'That's all nonsense. I knew Clyde better than anybody. If there were somebody like that, I would've known.'

'My point exactly, sir.' Wilma returned the stony stare and let a silence fall for a few uncomfortable beats. 'Mr. Chalmers, I stumbled upon a reference to a musician named Stacy Parker. It just strikes me as a fascinating coincidence. There's a stolen guitar involved in this case, and a woman maybe calling herself Stacy trying to reach the victim. And there's a man who I think knows a lot more than he's willing to tell me.'

That caused Chalmers to break into another smile, look down and shake his head. 'If you're thinkin' this ole country boy actually knows somethin', well, you're the first, lemme tell you.'

Charming or not, Wilma had finally had it from this character. 'Okay, how about we drop the 'aw-shucks ma'am' routine now, Mr. Chalmers? I have to tell you, you do lay it on *awful* thick. I've been a small-town girl my whole life and let me say, I'm kind of offended by it. You come off like a hillbilly from a TV show. And by the way, maybe you're from rural Tennessee, like you say, but I happen to know you're hardly an ignorant hick. For one thing, you spent two years at Vanderbilt University in Nashville. You studied business with a minor in English literature. I would guess you weren't *droppin'* an awful lot of your G's at the end of your words with your professors in those classes, now, were you?'

Chalmers took a deep breath but didn't look up or say anything. Wilma leaned in closer, speaking quietly but emphatically.

'One thing you've said that I can totally believe: you were closer to Clyde Claudebetter than anyone else. I think there *is* a mystery relative, I think she's connected to Clyde's death, and I think you know about her. So how about you stop play-acting the 'good ole country boy' role and stop insulting my intelligence and for once tell me the truth, Mr. Chalmers?'

The only part of him that moved were his clear blue eyes, rolling up at her from under the hoods of his thick eyebrows. It was a particularly long moment before the eyes perceptibly softened and he made his decision.

'I wish you could just leave her alone,' he said in a low voice. 'Lord knows, she's had enough trouble.'

6

It was a good hour before Wilma walked back out the door of Chalmers's cabin, her face ashen and her expression grim. Purvis did not see her to the door; he had remained sitting and simply said he figured she knew the way out. The story she had just heard made her head spin, and yet it all made sense and accommodated all the suspicions she had formulated. As she had listened to Chalmers, it all had just started falling into place.

She took out her phone and dialed Moon.

'Yes, Chief,' he sighed.

'Mr. Moon, is Nate Stillman still with you?'

'He's about to leave. He has to get back to his office to take care of the things we just discussed.'

'There's been a change of plans. As soon as he's gone, I'm going to need you to take that guitar back to where you found it right away, and please leave it out in the open.'

'What? Wait a minute, I thought you wanted me to keep it safe here at the house! What's going on?'

'As I said, there's been a change of plans. There's some new information. I know who killed Mr. Claudebetter and I'm pretty sure they'll be coming back for the guitar.'

'That sounds as if you don't suspect me anymore, then. That's a relief.'

'No, sir, I'm quite sure it wasn't you.'

'Then who was it?'

'I'll tell you the whole story once this is over, and I'm thinking it's going to be over sometime tonight. So would you please just bring the guitar back right away, and then return to the house and stay there until I contact you. Stay away from the garage and the apartment.'

'But . . .'

'Sir, that's all I can tell you right now. Once you've taken care of that for me, please just sit tight at the house until you hear from me.'

She terminated the call and started making a mental list of the people she needed to call and the preparations she needed to make. She figured she had a few hours yet, but there was a lot to be done, and she might only get one chance. Shortly thereafter, she saw Stillman's car on the road, heading back down the hill, as she rapidly spoke into her phone.

★   ★   ★

An hour or so after sunset, the Pumpkin Ranch looked thoroughly desolate. The stretch along State Road 86 was deserted. There was likely nobody around who would hear the crunch of tires on gravel as a lone vehicle pulled up at the dark driveway before the ranch entrance. The driver left the engine running, the car's headlights illuminating the locked gate, and exited the vehicle, walking to the electronic lock and keying in a code. The gate slowly opened with a creak. The figure returned to the car and drove through the gate, which automatically closed, and turned left onto the dark road to the garage.

The vehicle slowly approached the deserted garage and apartment building, the driver cautiously observing the scene. The police had long since departed. None of the staff would be on the premises this evening because of the events of the previous day. A couple of floodlights had been left on as usual in front of the buildings, but there were no other cars in sight and no lights on within either building.

It had turned out to be a fortunate chance they were taking. As expected, there seemed to be a window of opportunity that wouldn't last very long. There wouldn't be a better opening for what was needed to be done.

The driver pulled the car past the driveway, to the side of the garage, out of the light, and parked. The figure walked quickly and silently around to the apartment building, pulled a ring of keys from a pocket, opened the door and entered.

Once inside, they shut the door behind

themselves and produced a small flashlight. They knew exactly where they were going, and slipped upstairs and to the memorabilia room, where they furtively maneuvered around the various shelves, moving the small light back and forth. The object of the search was not to be found, but it had to be here somewhere — and they swore quietly to themselves, thinking where else to look. After perhaps ten minutes, they retraced their steps out of the room and back downstairs, then turned right to the access door to the garage, extracting the key ring and unlocking it.

The tiny light pierced the deep darkness of the garage as the figure moved around the Camaro and the Shelby Mustang, scanning the bare surroundings while heading towards the laundry door. The flashlight beam swept towards the door and caught a gleam of metal. Where the previous day a cheap plastic laundry basket had sat in front of the laundry door, there was now a rectangular guitar case, dark with silver corners, leaning on end against the wall.

The searcher hesitated, taken by surprise by this turn of events, then approached the case, turning it onto its side on the floor and opening it, the snaps making a noise that seemed loud in the eerie stillness of the garage. The flashlight beam swept over the butterscotch-blonde finish of the guitar in the case and settled on the head and the tuning pegs, the familiar stylized script *Fender*, and in smaller capitals, TELECASTER.

It was surprising to find it here, but it was what the seeker had come for, so the lid was closed, the locks were re-snapped, and the case was quietly lifted by its handle off the floor. The dark figure carefully maneuvered around the vehicles and back through the apartment foyer, relocking both doors, then began to briskly walk, guitar case in hand, across the front of the garage back to the parked car waiting in the shadows around the side.

It was when they had reached the car and popped the trunk, depositing the guitar case within, that they realized they were not totally alone. There was the sound of a woman clearing her throat from the darkness beyond, further toward the back of the garage.

'This time you found what you wanted, Stacy, am I right?'

The figure froze, but only for a moment, then reached up and slammed the trunk shut, peering into the darkness in front of the car.

'Chief Acosta? Is that you?'

'I figured you'd be coming back tonight for the Cray guitar. This would be the only chance you'd have.'

'I . . . I don't know what you're talking about. Who's Stacy?'

'Oh, come on. I know the whole story. I know why you came to the ranch to begin with. I know why you want the guitar. I'm pretty sure you didn't intend to kill Clyde. You just wanted the guitar, but that's what wound up happening. I'm afraid it's all over now, Stacy.'

The figure, backlit by the light from the driveway, stepped to the side of the car, a hand reaching beneath a jacket. 'I'm sorry. I didn't want any of this to happen. I don't want this to happen either.'

Wilma started to call out something, but before she could, Roy Bivins had pulled a revolver out of a shoulder holster and fired three times into the darkness.

There was a cry from Wilma. 'I'm sorry!' Bivins yelled again, but this time full of anguish and panic. He turned back and forth, trying to decide his next move: he thought about simply running but then realized he needed his car. He reholstered the weapon and frantically reached in his pocket for his car keys.

That was when the small red spot appeared on his chest and a male voice said, 'Hold it right there.'

Bivins started to move, but Jim Burton shouted out, 'I don't really need this laser sight. I'm a dead shot with this rifle and I can put three slugs into you before you can move, so I suggest you stop and get your hands in the air *now*.'

The chauffeur dropped the keys and did as told.

'Now, very slowly, hold your jacket open with your left hand and very slowly take out that weapon,' Burton barked. 'Thumb and forefinger on the edge of the grip. If I see a finger heading toward the trigger, I *will* shoot. That's good. Now gently toss it out there toward the driveway. Now get down on your knees and lace your fingers behind your head and then *do not move*.' As soon as Bivins had complied, Burton had flipped on his flashlight and was moving toward Wilma, who was now leaning against the garage.

'Chief! Are you okay?'

'I'm fine, Jim. She missed me completely twice and put one right through my shoulder with the third. Hurts, but I'll live. Go get some cuffs on her and we'll get the rest of the crew down here.'

As Burton took hold of Bivins's wrists and slapped then into handcuffs, the little chauffeur glared into the dark at Wilma. She walked forward into the light, holding a hand against her shoulder; and despite the pain shooting through her body, she noticed that tonight Roy Bivins' dapper perfectly trimmed mustache was missing from the perfectly smooth face.

'Chief, we need to get you immediate medical attention,' Burton said, not trying to hide the alarm in his voice. He was already grabbing the button on his shoulder radio. 'You're bleeding pretty good there.'

Wilma looked at the spreading red patch around the hole on her uniform shirt. 'Damn, she pretty much just grazed me. I felt the bullet exit right out again.'

Burton turned his attention to the walkie-talkie as it crackled to life. He called for backup and an ambulance on the double, then kept switching his attention back and forth between Bivins and Wilma, his expression growing more confused by the moment. 'Wait. So Roy Bivins is a *woman*? And that Mulier woman had nothing to do with this?'

'It's complicated,' Wilma sighed. 'Very complicated. As for Alia Mulier, well . . . you're looking at her right there as well.'

She ignored Jim's bugging-out eyes; she suddenly felt really tired and looked around for somewhere she could sit down.

7

'How are you feeling, Chief?' Marlowe Moon asked. 'Is that chair comfortable enough for you?' He was being particularly solicitous of her wellbeing at the moment, a surprising turn of events. Wilma was seated in an easy chair, her right shoulder bandaged and her arm in a sling, basking in the sunlight streaming into the parlor. She heard a clock in the kitchen chime brightly ten times. It was an incongruously cheery moment in the Claudebetter hacienda.

Wilma waved her good hand. 'I'm fine, Mr. Moon, thank you.'

'I appreciate your coming by this morning to tell this . . . remarkable story.'

'Afterward, I've got to sit in on an interrogation of the accused and then a short press conference, and then I'm told I have to leave everything else to everyone else. But I did promise to tell you the story, after all.'

He shook his head, looking very self-conscious. 'I can't believe I was so fooled. It's embarrassing.'

'Well, it seems as if everyone here was fooled. Nobody was really paying attention, and she took advantage of that.' Wilma was feeling a trifle magnanimous this morning. She had finally gotten some sleep, the pain killers seemed to be working, Moon was being actually human, and she had the chauffeur services of Clarence White, who would be returning for her as soon as she gave him a call.

'The one thing I still don't quite understand is how you could be so certain that Roy — I mean, Stacy — would be returning to the ranch last evening. It would have made more sense for him — I mean her — to pull up stakes and run right away.'

'The Cray guitar, Mr. Moon. It was all about the guitar. It stood to reason that she desired that guitar dearly. After taking that much of a risk and finding she had gotten the wrong one, she couldn't leave it behind. It was the only opportunity she'd get. You'd sent all the staff home, and from what she knew, I'd no longer need my deputies to be here. It'd be a different story the next day. There could be a ton of people around here dealing with Mr. Claudebetter's death. Not to mention, the longer she waited, the more chance that it would be discovered that the Cray guitar was still here in the wrong case, or that all the memorabilia would just be moved somewhere inaccessible. It *had* to be last night.'

'This is all so astounding . . . and so sad. Despite what she put us all through, I find myself feeling a terrible sympathy for Stacy Parker. She's a very gifted individual in so many ways, and her life's such a mess.'

'Yes, sir, I have to agree with that.'

She couldn't help but consider that one con artist would tend to admire the craft of another.

Moon sat back in his own chair, laced his fingers and shook his head slowly. 'So Stanley Parker had begun to realize he identified more as a girl than a boy, and his first big mistake was to feel he could confide that to the one person he trusted, Clyde Claudebetter.'

'It would seem Clyde couldn't handle that. Old macho country boy and all, it was too much for him. He tried to talk Stanley out of it but finally it all came to a major blow-up between them. That was the issue that split them apart for good.'

'Up until then, they had been so close, you say. Clyde took Stanley under his wing like a father to a son. He taught him how to drive and fix fast cars, how to play guitar, introduced him to the musical luminaries he counted as friends . . . and promised him that one day the Cray guitar would be his, is that right?'

'That all meant the world to Stanley,' Wilma said. 'His no-count father had left, his mother had died, and his relationship to Clyde was the most important thing he had. It was a short moment of happiness. I guess that guitar, and that promise, took on a special symbolism to him. Maybe because his own father was a musician as well. Well, I'm surely no psychologist.'

'So Stanley left and in due course became Stacy. She evidently had the musical gene from both sides of the family. She had some small success as a musician and was even a talented actor, it would seem.'

Wilma nodded. 'She was smart, she was talented, she taught herself about all sorts of things . . . as you said, a highly gifted individual. But doubtless, her life was not easy. She never again found anybody she could trust or rely upon. A hard knocks-existence to be sure.'

'And somehow at the very nadir of that existence,' Moon said, 'she stumbled upon Clyde and the Pumpkin Ranch and it all came back to her.'

'It's kind of ironic to me that she decided to take on the role of a male chauffeur and apply for work here. I don't think Clyde had any idea that Stanley had become Stacy.'

'She wanted to get to be his driver,' Moon said. 'It was the way she figured she could get closest to him. I think her instincts were right on. Clyde Claudebetter would never have hired a woman to drive him. He was too old-fashioned for that.'

'It was pretty outrageous how she got away with it, wearing that costume mustache, obtaining a fake driver's license and ID, talking in that low voice from the gut.'

Moon smiled grimly. 'But she's got a devastating sense of humor, I've got to give her that. She took a name that included Roy G. Biv — the Rainbow symbol, a reference to her gender switch. A joke that only she got, as it turned out.'

'There was actually one other person who got the joke, but let's come back to that. It's interesting that Clyde became quite fond of Roy Bivins, to the point of protecting the chauffeur's job and finding ways to keep Bivins on. It would seem on some level the affection for his nephew was still there, and he just couldn't acknowledge it.'

'For someone who's not a psychologist, you're doing one hell of a job, Chief.'

'Just trying to wrap my head around all this, Mr. Moon, to make some sense of it. I'm still not sure how much at first she was motivated by getting hold of that guitar and how much she just wanted to somehow reconnect with the person who had shown her the most kindness and love in her life.'

Moon leaned forward in his chair. 'I'm inclined to think it might have started as a way to reunite with Clyde, but when she saw how self-absorbed and distracted he had become, she gave up on him. With time it became an obsession to get the guitar. It stood for a broken promise she wanted made good. That would explain the phone calls as Stacy to try to talk to Clyde.'

'And then,' Wilma said, 'Roy Bivins's hours got cut back, so she hit upon an even wilder scheme. She became Alia Mulier and applied for the afternoon housekeeper's job. She wore a wig and heavy glasses and kept a low profile around the house. She gambled that nobody paid attention enough to catch on. I can't imagine how difficult that had to be, to lead two lives, to come and go twice a day.'

'More of her rapier wit,' observed Moon. 'Alia Mulier: Another Woman. Again, a joke nobody else got. She banked on the fact nobody would be paying close attention to her. Mr. Claudebetter was losing his sight and hearing and becoming increasingly distracted, and I . . . well, I was letting things get by me in ways I'm not proud of.'

'I wonder if she wanted to be found out. The joke names, the increasingly crazy complicated existence. Whatever, it would seem something had to give, and it finally did. Stacy took a big risk to go into the memorabilia room and grab that guitar. For some reason, she decided the other night would be the best opportunity. I'm a little unclear on the details as yet, but it would seem that after you left for the day, she made her move. I bet she went through the motions of leaving the ranch but didn't really. Instead she doubled back a little later, after she figured Chalmers had checked the garage on his rounds. She took the laundry basket just in case she might be seen and needed an excuse. Maybe she would've scrubbed the mission if that had been the case, but she figured she'd lucked out and hadn't been seen.'

'I don't understand why she opened the garage door and entered the apartment that way.'

'I'm guessing she couldn't risk taking the keys to the apartment and cast immediate suspicion on Alia. But Roy the chauffeur had the keys to the garage . . . and, unknown to anybody else, a key to the door leading from the garage to the apartment. So she entered the building through the garage, dumped the basket, and was smart enough to close the garage door behind her. She went up to the memorabilia room, and found what she thought was the Cray guitar. That's when things started to go wrong.'

'And when she came back, why did she back the Mustang out of the garage?'

'She didn't. I believe Clyde did that.'

'What?'

'Here's what I'm thinking. Clyde cooked an early dinner with Purvis Chalmers and it would seem they talked about cars, and likely the Shelby Mustang in particular. As you know, Clyde was prone to sentimental reminiscing of late, and maybe he was getting moony about that car of his. I'm thinking after dinner, Clyde got it in his head to walk down to the garage and maybe just take the car for a spin, even just around the property. He'd just backed the car out onto the drive-around and was walking back to close the garage door. That's when Alia came through the door holding the guitar case.'

Moon actually gasped. 'Good Lord. I can imagine the scene, if that's what happened.'

'It must have been pretty dramatic. Maybe everything finally came out between them. You can imagine they had quite the argument. Clyde would have tried to stop her from leaving and it would have gotten physical. Stacy, or Alia if you will, swung the guitar case and clobbered Clyde across the temple with it, he fell to the ground and hit his head, and that was that.'

Moon nodded. 'She had the presence of mind to pull the Mustang back into the garage and close and lock the garage doors.'

'But she forgot about the door from the

apartment building. She left that ajar.'

'What I don't understand,' Moon said, 'is how she got the wrong guitar after all that.'

'That was through the agency of someone else who figured out what was going on and was trying to prevent it.'

'You mean Purvis Chalmers?'

'Exactly. As you said, he's nowhere near as dull a tool as he likes to pretend. Chalmers picked up on what was happening pretty early in the game. He knew all along about Stanley becoming Stacy, and he figured out early in the game that Stacy was Roy, and then that she was also Alia. He never let on to anyone, not even Stacy, and certainly not Clyde. I think he kind of acted as her secret guardian angel now and then, behind the scenes. He worked out that she was planning to steal the Cray guitar and leave, and he knew how much that guitar meant to Clyde. To lose it would have broken his heart; in fact in the end he fought for it and it killed him. So Purvis snuck into the memorabilia room and switched cases with a cheap one, and then for good measure he hid the good guitar in the laundry room, locked the door, and fabricated the story about an out-of-order machine to keep anyone out of there.'

Moon's eyes lit up. 'Now that you mention it . . . yes, it could have been Chalmers who told me that the washing machine was broken and the room had been locked, not one of the housekeepers!'

Wilma nodded. 'He told me so himself. Purvis figured that Stacy was going to grab the guitar and leave and neither Roy nor Alia would ever be heard from again. It'd be a case of unreliable employees who had left without notice. Maybe Clyde and you would even think they ran off together, which would be quite an irony. He'd be able to retrieve the real Cray guitar and put it back in the collection and Clyde would be none the wiser.'

'But then Clyde showed up at just the wrong moment and got killed.'

'Unfortunately, yes.'

'Even after that tragic encounter, if she

had immediately fled and not returned, she could have gotten away.'

'And she might have had that exact idea in mind. I wouldn't be surprised if her car was already packed and ready to go right then and there. Or maybe she planned to run by the boarding house and pick up her things and leave town. In any case, after she left the premises, she must have opened the guitar case and realized she had the wrong guitar. After all she'd gone through, she couldn't just leave her prize behind. She knew she had to go back, and that meant carrying on in her role as Roy for another day, going in and opening up in the morning and 'discovering' Clyde's body and riding it out until she could get the guitar.

'Alia would have kept calling in sick as long as needed, maybe quit or gotten fired, and that identity would've been gone for good, but I threw a monkey wrench in *that* works when I had you call her in for questioning. She probably worried I might be a bit more observant than the usual occupants of the house, so she applied lipstick, powder and nail polish, covered herself in a hat and dark glasses, and put on an Academy Award performance as a sick woman.'

Moon, ever the germophobe, visibly shuddered at the memory. 'She certainly had me going with that act.'

Wilma tried to adjust her position in the seat and winced a little bit at a twinge of pain in her shoulder. 'My deputies and the Nightingale police found packed suitcases and Clyde's other guitar and case at Roy's boarding-house room last night, as well as Stacy's own guitar, a cheap acoustic model. Another roomer said that she played her guitar constantly, at a low volume since she didn't use a pick. That was what started to get me going, in fact, in the first place.' She waggled the fingers on her left hand.

'What do you mean?'

'I happened to notice that Roy Bivins had awfully well-manicured hands for a mechanic. And it was an odd manicure: on one hand the nails were long but trimmed very carefully, while on the other hand they were cut short. It's the way a guitarist who fingerpicks a lot might keep them.'

'Amazing!' said Moon, truly impressed.

'I have to thank my husband George for that insight. But stranger still, I happened to notice that Alia Mulier's nails, even though she took the trouble to paint them, were trimmed the exact same way. What would the odds be? Two people in two different walks of life and both fingerpicker guitarists! But even more curious, as I thought about it, they were around the same size and build . . . and their fingers were so similar in general that it was downright bothersome!'

'Very perceptive. So you deduced that Roy and Alia were the same person?'

'I didn't want to believe that at first, Mr. Moon. It was just too outrageous, like something you'd read in a book, you know? But with time, the evidence grew, and I finally had to accept the conclusion.'

'That's quite a piece of detective work, Chief. I'm very impressed. I must admit I misjudged you. I apologize.'

'Police work is like most other fields,

Mr. Moon. It's all about putting in the time and the effort until something works.'

'One percent inspiration,' Moon quoted, 'and ninety-nine percent perspiration. That was how Thomas Edison defined genius.'

'Is that so? I like that. But there was hardly any genius involved in this case.' She smiled slyly. 'Perhaps you've learned that you don't have to come from a big city to possess some level of native intelligence.'

Moon raised his eyebrows sheepishly and avoided her gaze. 'Touché, Chief, touché.'

Wilma let the moment pass. 'So what'll happen with the ranch?'

'That remains to be seen. It'll be Purvis's now. He'll probably keep the stablemen and the landscapers on, not to mention the housekeepers, but I can't see him wanting to keep me around.' Moon sighed deeply. 'My cover's going to be blown. This place was a sanctuary. Now I'm not sure what might come out about me.'

'Maybe nothing needs to come out. It would appear that Stacy Parker is going to make a full confession as part of a plea bargain. There may be no need to elicit testimony from you or implicate you. You might be free and clear.'

'That would certainly be a good turn of events. But I'll have to move on and find another safe harbor. I'm a survivor, Chief. I'll find a way.'

'Just a small suggestion, Mr. Moon. You seem to do better when you're sober, if you don't mind my saying.'

Moon simply nodded, silently and sadly.

★   ★   ★

'So, that medical degree you got that you never told me about?' George asked, looking up from the couch.

Wilma stopped dusting the table top and turned to him. 'What the devil are you taking about, George? What medical degree?'

'The one you apparently have that makes you think you know more than

Doctor Tanaka over at Amberville General Hospital. I mean, what with her telling you not to overexert yourself and keep resting up for another week or two, and what with you ignoring her, I have to figure you just got more of a medical education than she does.'

'George, I'm going stir crazy here. I can't sit still for another couple of weeks! I'm fine!' She turned partway and suddenly winced in pain, involuntarily reaching up to the sling across her bandaged shoulder.

'Uh-huh. Would you sit back down and stop trying to clean up around here?'

'Honestly, I don't know how you can sit and watch television so much. I'm bored silly!'

George patted the empty spot next to him. 'Come on, doctor's orders. You'll be healed before you know it and back to work.'

'That's another thing,' she huffed as she dropped herself into the cushions. 'Who knows how they're screwing things up at the station?'

'Now you know how I felt when I

retired and you took over.' George shot her a sly sideways glance. 'We all like to think we're not replaceable, darlin'. Fact of the matter is, we are. I'm sure Jim's running things just fine in your absence. And he's got Natalie, who really runs the place to begin with.'

'I know, I know. I've checked in a few times this week . . . '

'I know you have. You're probably driving them crazy over there. Leave them be.'

'But what if something comes up?'

'You mean like another locked-room celebrity murder with multiple zany suspects? Wouldn't you say one of those every few decades is enough to expect in Amberville? I suspect they can deal with the speeders, drunks, shoplifters and teenage vandals for a while longer. You and I both know the department can almost run itself most of the time.'

'Way to make a girl feel good about herself,' Wilma muttered.

The news had come on the television station they were watching, with footage of Holly Travers standing in the roadway at the front entrance to the Pumpkin Ranch.

'How long are they going to try to milk this one?' George wondered. 'There's nothing really new, just a report every few days saying 'Nothing new's happening.''

'I guess Ms. Travers is worried we'll all forget her.'

'So what *is* happening at the ranch, I wonder?'

'Last I heard was from Diego, when he called last week.'

'Nice of him to do that. He always struck me as a decent sort.'

'That he is. Anyways, he said that Purvis Chalmers called the ranch hands and the gardeners together and told them he was keeping them all on. The housekeepers too. At least for now. All the cars are being put up for auction, and Diego figures the garage and the apartment are going to be closed up. Purvis isn't one for cars. He'll keep his old jeep up at the main house and that's all he'll need. But Diego thinks that ultimately Purvis is going to sell the whole thing, maybe with a stipulation that the buyer retain the employees, and he'll move back to Tennessee. There's really nothing to keep him here. That's all I know.'

'Any idea what became of that Moon guy?'

'Nope. Diego said he was gone already. Once the prosecutor's office told him he wouldn't be required to testify and was free, he was in the wind.'

'Didn't you say he was the executor of the estate?'

'He signed off on that in favor of Nate Stillman, if you can believe it. Wanted to get away from there as fast as possible, it would seem. He's got something coming from the inheritance, so I'm sure Nate knows where to find him, for now at least.'

'So the niece spilled everything. I'm kinda surprised.'

'I think she was haunted by everything that happened. That's a pretty deep and complicated relationship she had with Claude. That guitar was awfully important to her, and he'd hurt her deeply way back, but in the end she didn't want anything bad to happen to him. The fact she killed him, well . . . that seems to have messed her up pretty badly.'

George shook his head. 'I'm still trying to wrap my head around that. So *he* became a *she* and then pretended to be a *he* . . . Just how far did she take that change? I mean, did she . . . you know . . . ?'

'I haven't asked and I'm sure I'll find out, but I don't really care, George. Does it really matter? She felt she was a woman so she lived as one. That's all I need to know as far as the murder case went. All the rest I'll leave to the Holly Traverses of the world.'

'Does she have any family, friends, anybody?'

'Not that could be found. She was pretty much a loner.'

'Damn,' muttered George, shaking his head again. 'Poor woman. Surely had the deck stacked against her from the cut and deal, wouldn't you say?'

'I would, yes,' Wilma said, reaching for the remote for the TV. 'Anything on besides the news? For some reason I don't want to watch that.'

As George predicted and Wilma feared, all went smoothly in her absence as Amberville police chief. She was two weeks returned to her post when she got the call from Nate Stillman.

'Chief, I heard you were back on the job. How are you feeling?'

'Better every day, thanks, Mr. Stillman. What can I do for you?'

'I thought I'd bring you up to date and inform you that the Claudebetter estate has been settled and all distributions made. The auctions went quickly and successfully; I'm sure the notoriety didn't hurt. There were numerous people across the country interested in the Mustang and the guitars especially, and selling action was brisk.'

'People can surely have a ghoulish side. They wanted something that was connected to a sensational murder, did they?'

'It would seem so. Purvis Chalmers is now officially in possession of the Pumpkin Ranch, with a quite respectable bank account. A disbursement was made to Marlowe Moon ... to a bank in Honolulu, I might add. It would seem that our friend has landed on his feet in Hawaii. I'm expecting to have no further communications from him.'

'Good for him, I suppose. I hope he keeps his nose clean, and I guess I wish him well, but I'd be just as happy to not hear from him again either.'

'Mr. Chalmers has asked me to remain as attorney for the ranch for now and deal with any administrative issues that arise. I'm guessing his ultimate goal will be to sell the place, but right now he feels he's got a responsibility to the staff. He's just going to tread water until he and they can all formulate other plans.'

'That was what I figured as well. He can return home and live pretty comfortably from now on.'

There was a short awkward silence on the other end of the phone. 'Well ... I just wanted to bring you up to date, Chief. Please let me know if I can be of any further assistance to you.'

'Sounds like you're busy, Mr. Stillman. Well ... *ave atque vale.*'

'Excuse me?'

'That means goodbye, right? One of my deputies studied Latin back in the day. He was actually in the seminary at one point. He told me to tell you that if I ever got the chance.'

'Well, not the usual context but . . . close enough. Goodbye.'

Wilma got her wish. It would be the last she would ever hear of Marlowe Moon.

The conversation with Stillman got her to thinking. She reached across her desk to her old-fashioned Rolodex and flipped the cards until she reached the one with a business card taped onto it: Detective Frank Vandegraf.

She picked up her phone and juggled it in her hand, contemplating whether she should give him a call and tell him the story. She couldn't think of anyone who would believe it or appreciate it more.